# MALICE IN BLUNDERLAND

# MALICE IN BLUNDERLAND

## JONNY GIBBINGS

**A Cutting Edge Press Paperback Original**

Published in 2011 by Cutting Edge Press

www.CuttingEdgePress.co.uk

Copyright © Jonny Gibbings

**ISBN: 978-1-908122-12-4**

I want 'Malice' to be as if you've found someone's diary on a park bench. Within it spews the darkest, most intimate, personal thoughts. Written in the heat of the moment. Voyeuristic and intimate. Unpolished, unedited, with all the raw jaggy sharp edges. As if you somehow found yourself inside the head of a guy in melt down, vision and competence obscured by drugs, pain and exhaustion.

*Jonny Gibbings*

# ACKNOWLEDGMENTS

To Josh Hay, for picking 'Malice' up, believing in me and making it happen. And putting up with all my shit. To Paul Swallow, for having the gayest name, and for fine tuning my work and to both Paul and Josh, for without a doubt, making the ending work better and holding true to the spelling concepts. To All at Cutting Edge Press - Martin, Helen, Melody and Marissa - for your bravery and vision. To CJ, an inspirational guy who reminds me to never give up. To Richie Price, for still finding my shit funny after all these years and pushing me to start. To James Hawker of Future Waveski's and Luke Yong surfboards for all the free shit.

To all of the above, a massive thank you. To Kai and Ella, thank you for giving me a reason to straighten up. When you are old enough, I hope you find 'Malice in Blunderland' funny

Lastly, to Sophie. For your integrity, patience, forgiveness, honesty, putting up with a disaster like me. But mostly for teaching me love isn't finding the person you can live with. It's finding the person you can't live without.

Oh, lastly, to Bulldog, sorry for the pubes in your sandwich, it was me.

# Warning

Spelling Mistakes, ~~Miss-use~~ Misuse of
Punctuation & Grammer is intentional!

If idiosyncratic righting offends...

## Look Away Now

# CHAPTER 1

**Sunday**

# 1

I hear voices. I open my eyes in a panic because I think they are coming to get me. I've always had paranoid delusions that people are after me. It is pitch black and I hold my breath to better listen to the voices. They're happy voices and so is ok, it seems its just a family talking about their holiday. Happy voices. I fucking despise happy people. But I live alone so what the fuck is a family doing in my flat?

I sit up, eyes slowly adjusting to the dark and it's happened again. I'm not in my flat, I'm in a tiny 'V' shaped room and I have no idea where I am. This has been happening a lot lately. Not waking up in 'V' shaped rooms, but waking up in strange places. Other people's houses, sheds, toilets where a tramp has used my trouser leg to wipe his ass, a brick factory, a wheelie bin. I'm a bit like Sam Beckett from that TV show 'Quantum Leap' where he time travels and has to work out who he is. I'm like the real life, low-rent scum version. Unlike Sam, I don't actually travel through time. I just drink till I pass out, and swallow as many drugs as I can to numb the pain. I'm not talking pop star lifestyle. No champagne and cocaine here and I'm no Kate Moss either. This is Tenants Super and Ketamine. We're talking proper low-rent. I have all the class of farting during sex. This isn't for a party lifestyle neither, we're talking basic survival here, just to function. Just to make it through another shit fuelled day. As a result, more often than not I wake up, in strange places with pockets full of stolen stuff. Not good stuff either. Photos of families still in the frame, someone else's contact lenses, athletes foot cream, TV remote controls, kids toys, a packet of ham, tampons. I tell lies too. I must hate the real me so much that I tell lies. I go to bars and laugh with people I don't know. Answer to the first name they call me. Pretend to be a friend of a friend and crash their parties. I steal their tampons and their ham. I put photos of other peoples families on their mantle. I'm the mess at every function, every party. I'm the fucker who makes a seen and embarrasses everyone. I'm the guy you think about taking outside and giving a kicking to, but your wife or girlfriend feels sorry for me and grabs your arm and tells you to 'leave it'. That's me.

I've had so many lie-jobs. Photographer, insurance broker, vet. I have discovered people don't listen or actually give a fuck who you say you are anyway. So my pretend jobs have become more and more bizarre, a proctologist, gay bar owner, dungeon slave. The temporary party friendship, where they want to associate with a better class of person and will believe anything you tell them, in the temporary suspended reality of temporary friends. Witty anecdotes, fake laughs and fake relationships.

3

"Hi I'm Clara, I'm here with Milly. Didn't I see you at her wedding?"

"Yep." *(nope)*

"So how do you know Milly and Steve?"

"Went to school with Steve." *(The 'went to school with' never fails)*

"Cool, cool. So, what do you do?"

"What do you think I do?" *(answer questions with questions)*

"Youuuuu, look like a... vet/proctologist/accountant etc?"

"Well done, that's right."

Job done, your in. A pseudo friend. Drink their drinks, take their drugs, steal some shit. Oh and find their toilet. Go for a luxury shit, nothing like laying one in some else's toilet. Everyone else's toilet is much nicer than mine. Mine doesn't have a pine scent or pretty paper. Mine's got dried piss all over it and is covered in so much pubic hair it looks like it has grown a beard. I have developed a party habit here too, I never flush. I want people to walk in from their fun, fun, fun, party and see a bowl of my steaming fresh shit. A cynical reality check. A calling card if you like, informing them that someone at the party is a filthy fuck. Its my art, my special party gift. Installation art. My illustration of the world as I see it – a bowl of shit. I don't use paper neither, I don't want anything to hide my work. My naked shit. So I wipe my ass on the towel, so even after someone has flushed my art, they can still smell it. They can wear it on their face if they use the towel in the morning.

Things are becoming clearer. My 'V' shaped room is actually a boat. I'm in a fucking boat! I'm not sure if I can swim, or I can't remember if I can. How did I get in a boat? Also, what were the voices? Mermaids? My eyes have adjusted and I'm bathed in a strange dark green light so I can only see shapes and shadows. I don't know who I was, where I am or who's boat this is. What I do know is I have no shoes on. This means one of two things. I've had sex or been for a shit. I can't do either with shoes on. I'm not sure why. I've been that way since I was a small kid. Having to take my shoes off for a shit that is, not the having sex bit. I wasn't trying to fuck people as a little kid with shoes on. But there must be a link. So far then I might have had sex, been for a shit and I might have stolen a boat. I don't know where I am or who I am meant to be. I am hoping I had sex. God I need it to be sex. To be deemed fuckable, that would be pretty solid gold good. I make my way over plastic patterned waterproof cushions, a small broken table, through the stink of booze breath to find the exit of the boat covered in green tarpaulin. That explains the lighting situation then. I slug my way under it to get off the boat, and to my surprise, its in a car park, surrounded by other boats. On stilts. And the owners of the voices are getting them ready to go in the water for summer. I must have climbed in for somewhere to sleep. So that's that mystery solved. But where the fuck am I? In a big boat-filled car park by a river? I search for a ladder down, and find one of my shoes, next to a big pile of shit. So that answers that mystery too then, there wasn't any sex.

5

The disappointment is huge and for a second I get that pre-cry lump building up in my throat. I find my way off the boat. I didn't find the other shoe but did find one sock. I feel like boiled crap, and start my walk home. After ascending a massive hill, like I was walking up to Heaven, a hill called Bonfire Hill that seemed to go on forever, I see a sign at the top where it meets a main road. 'Welcome to Salcombe – please drive slowly through the village'. So, Salcombe then. A long way from Plymouth. I don't know much, but I'm confident not many drivers will pick up a still drunk, one shoed hitch hiker. So, for what feels like a lifetime I do the long walk home. A couple of hours in, when I thought I might die of hunger, I find another shoe. I have often wondered why you see one abandoned shoe at the side of the road. I think maybe it's owner, like me, is having a breakdown and his way of manifesting his contempt and anger of the world is to toss his shoe out of the car window on the way to work. *"Shoes? SHOES? Yeah work, well fuck you, fuuuck you. I'm tossing a shoe, just one shoe at you work. How do you feel about that, eh work?"* Still his loss is my gain. I've one casual white skater style shoe and one slug eaten brown leather brogue, two sizes too big and no laces.

Did I say breakdown? I think I am having a break down, I always imagined a break down would be sudden, like when a car breaks down. Your OK then snap, you are in crisis with a drink and drug problem. Not a slow erosion. Like I was once a new proud snowman with a hat, scarf, carrot nose and smiley coal mouth. The pride of some little girl who soon gets bored of you, forgets you. And then there you are, alone. Thawing slowly over a period of days, becoming shapeless. Other kids punch your face off, a bird steals your nose, dogs piss up you and soon you are a dirty stinky puddle of mud and dog piss.

In my case, the little girl was called Mia. She was 22 when we met, and 32 when she left. If you read this Mia, this is ALL YOUR FAULT. Everything is your fucking fault. You did this. You let a dog piss me into a puddle and a bird steal my nose.

The description of you *is 'Cuntess'* Its not a word, but its the best I can do.

At about a quarter past fuck knows, I get back to my flat. I'm exhausted. Everything aches and my right foot is blistered to hell from the foreign oversized brown shoe. I'm so hungry I have a low sugar shake that would put Michael J Fox to shame. My hands were shaking so much that I thought it would be a shame to waste it and I considered masturbating but had to get in my flat first. After too many attempts I get the key in the lock and into my flat and am immediately plunged into darkness. I flick the light switch and nothing. So the electric has run out. It's dark outside and the only light I have is a battery powered Barbie lamp that I stole from a party once and my phone.

I walk over the floor carpeted with clothes and take away boxes, to the kitchen. Past the over flowing stink of the bin and the small carrier bags around the bin, also full of crap. To the cow cookie jar. I feel pain and that means the numbness is subsiding. I don't want to feel. I don't want to think. I don't want my throbbing foot pain, my hunger pain or the hurt of thinking of you Mia. And inside the cookie jar is my escape.

Ketamine. A tiny plastic bag of Ketamine. Not the little pink recreational ones with an apple on them. No these are the fuck off, white pills like giant asprin. We're talking proper horse stuff. Shut down your whole limbic stuff, take you to Disney World, paint some relief over my taught canvas of hurt stuff. Along side that is another little bag with speed in it. All this is thanks to my dealer and not really a friend, more a co-dependant, called Bulldog, who works in dispatch of the distribution area where I work.

I don't have depression, I have apathy I think. It's like a destructive anger but without enthusiasm. It's like rage if it took valium. They say apathy is an emotional response, but I think it is a medical condition like depression but the medical world hasn't caught on, so I self medicate. Also I am suffering from PMT (Post Mia Trauma). And the only cure for that is to try and fuck away the pain. However, vagina is harder to score on the street than any drug I know of. Well, it is if your a broke, alcohol bloated, small cocked, flappy titted fuck with a massive forehead like me. How you ever fucked me Mia I will never know.

My drug use isn't recreation like I've said. It is to exist, to get me through the day to day dross that is my life, or rather the lack of it. I use like M.S. sufferers use cannabis.

8

When Mia left, I couldn't sleep in between my pathetic displays of begging for Mia to take me back, crying outside her window. I mean full on snot bubble crying. I'd stay up and watch TV. I'd come home from work, eat dry cereal out of the box and just sit there, right through the night and go to work in the morning. Still in the same clothes. Each day I went to work I was more exhausted. Bulldog, found me sleeping by the bins outside and offered me some help. Speed. Or as he called it *"U.P.S. Beauties, beats, pep-pils, bumblebees, hearts, dexy. Phet, Billy, Whizz, Sulph, Base you know, a co-pilot."* I never thought I'd be a drug user, but the military used to give Benzedrine to it's soldiers for survival you know. One even walked across a whole dessert. And this was a similar situation. So, now I'm awake for 48 hours at a time, with all the pain of heartbreak. I'd go out and try to get laid, but I stink of desperation and loneliness. So, to take away the pain, I consulted Bulldog, my street doctor again. "Gimmie something else." I levelled with him, told him the situation. "Give me something that will num my whole fucking head," I said. He looked at me puzzled so I grabbed him and said "I want a fucking lobotomy."

So then came Ketamine. Special K. After all, this is for survival. So I don't feel anything anymore. I've been using for what seems like forever, and I only ever think about you Mia when the tide goes out, revealing raw nerves. So I take more and my chemical ocean rushes in and drowns my thoughts and floods my pain.

So here I am, one shoe mine, one anonymous shoe, blisters, empty stomach and one bastard of a hang over. I have some bread that might be mouldy, a fridge that isn't working because of no electricity, so I couldn't cook anything even if I wanted to. Even if I harvested some pizza carcases off of the floor.

Time for a *'kayvation'* as I call it. It isn't a word, but it is the best I can do.

I lie back on the sofa and drop a K with a swig of half a can of stale warm larger. In moments a hot feeling grows in my belly. Not long now and I won't have to think or feel. The numbness express is on time. Everything tingles, kaleidoscopes in my eyes, I can hear my heart sing instead of beat like a drum. Soon, I am part of the sofa as I dissolve into it, painted with Barbie light. No pain.

# 2

## Monday Boozeday

I wake in darkness, fumble about for my phone to check the time, 11.08. Still night. It seems like I've been asleep forever. I feel heavy. I also need a piss. So I stumble over the clothes and the daylight blazing in through the bathroom window hurts my eyes. Onward to the toilet with my morning wood, about to spray the walls. One eye closed, the other squinting I make it to the toilet and piss over it rather than in it.

Daylight? What the fuck? Why the fuck is the sun shining at night? I pat myself down to find my phone. It's on the sofa. I run back to the sofa and can't find the damned phone. I draw back the curtains and fill the ugly, filthy room with light. Through the dust in the air I see my phone and there it is 11.17am. Fuck I'm over two hours late.

I hate my job. Well that isn't quite true, I have manufactured something amazing, through pure apathy. I hate the company, the building, the cunts that work there. I despise everything about them and their little lives. But what I have managed to become, is without a doubt the most perfect evolution. I'm like the uvula. That hangy ball at the back of your throat. See, you didn't know it had a name did you? And thats my point. Me, I'm like your uvula. Never or rarely sees daylight, does fuck all, nobody knows what it does or why its there so they forget about it. No one has ever thought, I'd better clean my uvula or take it for a check up at the doctor. If it rotted and fell off, nobody would give a fuck. That's me. The companies uvula.

Let me tell you about Colorpure. No 'u' in colour, coz they are American. Their motto is there is no 'u' in colorpure – only 'we'. But there is, there is a 'U' in the pure bit you fucking idiots. I wouldn't mind so much if they said 'There is no U in our colour." That way, when ever a senior executive says it, I wouldn't find myself searching for something sharp to murder the fucker with. I have visions, me screaming, "There is a U in murder you fuckless fuck, this is for your own good," and bludgeoning his throat with a Colorpure company pen. A crimson fountain showers me and I look like a tomato with teeth. The office stands up to applaud and then we all run free like animals escaping a science lab.

On the first floor is the sales offices. Through the stainless steel and cream reception, with the so, so beautiful Marie Claire. Porcelain skin set with electric blue eyes. Everything perfect, nails, hair, shoes, like a man-made fuck-toy. A tiny waist over burdened by a set of massive, tits, only just secreted behind a silk blouse. When a Director, or successful sales rep, sorry, Colorpure Facilitator, walks through reception they get a full teethy smile and pouty full lips. An erection inducing fake laugh to go with the cursory greeting, "Morning – good weekend?" Or "Morning, love the tie." Me? Oh I'm just a call centre monkey on the technical response department. Like ghosts, if we walk through sales reception she looks right through us. Often she doesn't even bother to look up. There is no way us minions would register on her radar.

The first floor, is also the 'facilitators' floor. Open plan rows of desks and sales managers offices. Full of high fives, woops and big collared shirts. All clones to the 'Top Guns'. Oh yeah, I aint fucking kidding. The top sales guys get Top Gun status, and a framed certificate on their desk for proof. Probably mankind's best illustration of how to be a winner and a looser, at the same time. There is even a 'This months top, Top Gun'. Each desk has a cursory customization. Teddy bears to humanize it, pictures of family, flowers with complicated names. Each rectangle of desk is also a conflict zone with it's neighbour. On the walls are motivational pictures of beautiful inspiring landscapes, with captions below of fierce business. The irony is lost of how nature and industry are not happy bedfellows. The Top Guns dress all flashy like and all those below them copy their dress. Then there are the Sales Managers, the suits. Top Guns that have evolved into a higher grade of cunt. These give shit to the Top Guns, who give shit to those below them.

13

You should here these pricks talk about their jobs. They love it, trying to hit targets to go to the American head office. Are you kidding me? Work extra hard, give up your own time, to win the chance to fly over to America and do the exact same thing over there as you do here. Not like the fucknuts get to see any of America. They see the inside of a train, the inside of a plane and the inside of an identical office, but thousands of miles away. They come back and say it was amazing. *Is anyone fucking home?*

They come in early, go late, take work home and destroy their relationships. So that ultimately they have affairs at work. Then relationships with those at work. The parasite to the soul has got you, like that bit in the Matrix where Neo is in the battery of goo. You have become an ancillary. Part of Colorpure. Till they chuck you out like a spent Duracell.

Above them is the directors floor. Obviously, I have no fucking idea what that looks like, but it does have a massive guests area and conference room. Behind that, next to the emergency stairs is a bank of toilets. I spend pretty much all of my time in these toilets, they are like mini spa's. I will get to that in a second.

Like I say, I work in technical support. We sit at cubicles. Everyone has a cubicle and has taken to printing out and pinning their own inspirational motto to it. *"Let your advanced worrying become advance thinking and planning..."*, *"Life is not measured by the number of breaths we take, but by the moments that take our breath away..."*

and *"Imagination is more important than knowledge..."*. Mine says, *"If you can read this, you are already dead."* We all have headsets and take calls from irate customers complaining that when they update a bit of software, nothing else works. The usual, we have the latest operating systems and software crap. Make no mistake, Microsoft, Adobe and the likes are in one big cartel. A secret pact forcing you to upgrade and upgrade. Spend and spend. Colorpure sells large format printers and computer programmes to litho, offset printers and photographers. My job is to help customers with colour, sorry, color. Calibrating the systems to ISO or FOGRA, RGB to CMYK. for different usages and provide solutions when it doesn't work. You don't need to know fuck all, just read off the computerised script. You start the call with a 'Hello' then give your name and the reference number of the call, talk them into an information cul-de-sac so then they have to call sales for an upgrade.

It is a hate filled job in a hate filled office. We are on the ground floor, mirrored glass on the outside so nobody can see the captive and combined breaking of spirit and dignity but hey, we can see the directors car park. Not by accident. No,no,no. To inspire you to work hard, follow your dream. Own a BMW M5 like a director and you will be whole – complete. Trapped more like, forced to work to pay for shit you don't need, more like. Its like subconscious advertising, 'Hey, come get snared up like me'.

The turnover of employee here in technical support is amazing. Three months is the average. They come in all bright and bouncy, not Marie Claire bouncey, just full of enthusiasm. Having swallowed the pre-employment pep-talk of trips to America, the working their way up to the first floor, the company cars they could drive if they worked here for the rest of their lives. But reality is like the cancer we have in all of us, malignant and destructive. It will not be long before all the screaming, angry, ripped off customers calling you everything under the sun all day, every day will make you snap. One too many vile and abusive tirade and snap. Everyone snaps. And soon you will scream back, "Yeah, well fuck you too buddy – FUCK YOU!" Followed by the slam of a phone. On the other end of the call, when terminated, the customer is given an automated message, 'Was this call helpful? Press 1 for yes, 2 for no and 3 if you feel the advisor was rude.'

Amazingly, they can't calibrate your performance in technical support as you don't actually do anything constructive. You don't help anyone, you just spin them to upstairs to the sales floor. Here, performance is a negative calibration – how bad you do. If the customer doesn't hit a key in reply you are okay, and they don't care about the 1's but if you get to many 2's and 3's you get the sack. You're outta there. You leave the prison. So why the fuck, do so many cry and beg for another chance and promise to do better?

I wasn't aware of this little gem when I started, but then kind of lucked into a situation. My day is, clock in, go to my work station, turn it on, go to the coffee machine so my line manager sees me. Then sneak off up the emergency stairs to the customer toilets. To the mini spa. I take any bottles of water I can find and snacks I can steal from peoples desks on the way. The first thing I do, and the highlight of my day is a game 'Beat the fan'. I take my shoes off, in case I actually do need to take a shit, drop my trousers and sit on the pan. As soon as you walk in an extractor fan comes on, and stays on for about two and a half minutes, to suck out the shit-stink for the directors or customers. Not me, I see it as a challenge. To wank and blow my load before the fan cuts out. This might sound easy, but trust me it's not. The fan is on as soon as the door is open. It isn't a sportsman, it won't wait for a 'ready, steady – GO' its straight on. I have to get my shoes off, get my trousers down, then, depending how hung-over or tired I am there can be a good 20 seconds of wagging my cock about to get it hard. Then I have to buff away like I'm trying to start a fire. Fist a blur. I have to think of filthy shit to make me want to cum, and now and then, Mia, you sneak in my fantasy by accident and I lose my erection and have to start again. Finally I stand up to shoot my load. The fan wins some times. But when I win, it's a minor victory in a life of failure. Then I sleep. Right there on the pan. Sometimes I will drop a K and lose a day. If I do make an appearance, I sit at my workstation and watch porn. But, like so many modern technical companies, they run a filter that can detect the colour of human flesh. It is a sophisticated programme we were warned of. So I watch Henti Porn.

17

Japanese manga cartoons of real hardcore, massive cock and gaping arse filth. Like Pokemon, but with sex. After a bit of Henti its time to return to the toilet-spa for another wank and a sleep.

Turns out, this is excellent for my career, or lack of. I don't pick up the phone at my station as I'm not there. I'm wanking next door to the bosses or watching cartoon orgies. So I don't get any 2's or 3's. By accident, and by doing absolutely nothing, I am the top technical support technician. Not that I will become any sort of Top Gun, what with my ambition and the turn over of victims so high. Just means I'm not as shit as the other shits. As we are the bottom feeders I don't register on anyone's radar except for Mr Peterson. My line manager. Who, for as long as I can remember wears the same thing every day. Turns out he has 30 identical ties, multiple identical suits, sets of identical shoes, identical everything. He does not have an ounce of individuality at all. I found this out once in our kitchen area when someone knocked his lunchbox and it spilled on the floor. I picked up the plastic bagged sandwich and it was frozen. Then it was explained to me about Mr. Peterson's OCD. He makes up 31 identical sandwiches, just cheese, and freezes them at the beginning of the month. So each day is identical.

He is the sort of guy that will snap one day, and shotgun up the office. What a way to go, killed by an angry nerd. I will know exactly what my killer looked like, cyan blue tie, royal blue pinstripe suit, powder blue shirt and blue-framed glasses. All that blue, if that isn't a sign of impending disaster and death then I don't know what is.

I have been trying to force him to snap, push it along a bit. So some mornings, I take his frozen sandwich and place it in the ice maker compartment of our little office fridge, and at 12, I sneak back and put it back in his lunchbox. I sit in our lunch area and see him bite into a frozen, brick like sandwich. *"It's still frozen. Still frozen, I don't understand, I, I don't understand,"* he says every time, muttering under his breath and his face is a mix of confusion, disappointment and hunger. Other times I just remove the cheese. I swear I hear him think *"Who's Moved My Cheese?"* His eyes squint as he scans the room for the culprit. If you look hard, but you have to use your peripheral vision to see it, you can see Peterson tremble with rage. Small things I know but the cumulative effect is massive. He will snap one day. I'm sure of it. Ok, I know it sounds a bit weird but I have considered suicide more than once but I know I am too much of a coward to do it. To be the victim of an office killing would be brilliant. I just have to find some way of letting him know it's me, so I'm guaranteed he singles me out. I have a vision of a man in different shades of blue kicking down my partition and, with open arms, I'd embrace the shotgun. A crimson fountain showers from me and I look like a tomato with teeth. The office stands up to applaud and then all run free like animals escaping a science lab. To be assassinated, that'd be well cool. I may replace the cheese with a post-it note saying it was me, just to force it along. Imagine my fathers reaction when the police knock on the door "It's about your son, I'm sorry to tell you, but, he's been assassinated." There can be no better 'fuck you dad' than that.

I call it *'Blueicide'*. It's not a word, but it's the best I can do.

I'm already dressed, as I slept in my clothes. I smell worse than a wet dog. Getting close to 11.30 and I cant find my other shoe. I'm tossing the flat like a burglar on speed. Then I find the alien brown brogue and remember. Fuck – so now I have to start the process again but for shoes I know I have in a pair. A while longer than it should have taken, I'm up running for a bus, trying to use my phone at the same time. The long walk yesterday is making my legs protest. I can't risk getting sacked from this perfect job. My dependency is expensive.

"Bulldog – you gotta help me – punch me in."

"Where the fuck did you go last night dude? I ..."

Panting like Rolf Harris, I cut him off ,"Punch me in, punch me in."

"What? You aint at work?"

I can't breathe. "No... Punch... punshmeyinn."

"Dude, do you want me to punch in your card for you?"

I stop, bent double, hands on my knees. Feels like I have run a marathon, but from between my legs I can still see my front door. This was pathetic. "Yeah, yes... please mate."

"I was waiting for you this morning with your shit."

I'd forgotten I'd bought more speed. "Oh, okay, can you punch in my card though mate?"

"Did, waiting for you to turn up, you clocked on at 8.50 my friend."

"Oh, thank fuck. This speed shit doesn't work," I said

"What?"

"I can't run fast at all."

I get to my desk, heart still trying to punch it's way out of my chest, I boot up my work station, snatch a beaker of water from the cubicle beside me and drink like I've just been rescued from the Sahara. A fat, nameless girl goes to protest but sees my red sweaty face, spilled drink all down my chin and shirt, reeking of stale sweat and booze and panting like a paedophile at a kids party. She looks at me and I look at her and hope she doesn't cause a scene. I try to smile, but have a mouth full of her water, so am nose breathing like a raging bull. I try to hold my breath to look less like a mad man, but cant. I violently exhale and blow a massive slug like snot down my chin. I swallow the water and smile, with a snot chandelier hanging from my teeth.

Eventually I make it to the emergency exit, to the stairs and into the toilet. The fan comes on, shoes off trousers down. But I am exhausted. I think, 'Fuck you fan – you win.' I sit there, with my heart rate slowly returning. I rummage in my pockets as I know I will need something, to day of all days to get me through. Two pills. One speed, one Ketamine. *'Neo, in my hands I have two pills, a blue one and a red one.'* I know I should take the speed. I need to get through the day but I am exhausted. So I drop the K. I don't know if it was the heart rate returning, relaxing from the physical exertion, but it felt like an invisible hoover sucked my soul right out of my mouth. Like I was being melted in a microwave, my eyes rolled up in my head and that was it, a chemical coma.

Again, I wake up confused and not in my bed. Not a 'V' shaped room this time though. White tile walls, vaguely familiar white tile walls. Then I remember. It's dark and I'm still in the fucking toilet-spa. I check my phone and its just coming up to nine. My head feels like it has treacle in it as I make my way to my work station and shut it down. The cubicles look alien now that they are deserted and in darkness. I go and clock out and make my way to the technical response exit through reception that leads into the car park. As I get to the door there is a voice behind me. "Ahh, and what might you be doing here so late?"

I turn and standing there is, well I have no idea who the fuck he is, a Sales Manager or Director maybe. Too old for the sales team. He has salt and pepper hair and his hands and face are the same colour as the shoe I found in Salcombe. Brogue face walks towards me, blinds me with his teeth and prompts again, "Well?"

*Fuck, lie, lie you idiot – you do it all the time.* But I do a Madame Tussauds and just stand there looking at him with a wide eyed expression.

"Mr. Ell-ee-yot?" he phonetically spelt the name as he fired a one eye squint, to further illustrate the guess.

*Answer to the first name they call you.* "Yeah."

"Burning the midnight oil eh Mr. Elliot?"

"Ah, you know, some people are busy so I sometimes call them back outside of working hours, so I can give our customers the time they deserve." I cannot believe that shit came out of my mouth. I know I needed to come up with something but I feel sick that I could even think such bullshit. I hate myself and reach for the door. "Wait!" and the rythem of leather sole on marble floor approaches me. I'm afraid to look around as right there I imagine some bodysnatcher, mind melt. He will dislocate his bottom jaw like an egg eating snake and swallow my head. He'll stick his tongue in my ear, making me one of them. Implanting a Colorpure brain. "We could do with more like you in support. Go Getters, Company Men. You are coming for a drink with us and I won't hear a no." What the fuck?

In no time at all, I'm a passenger in a giant Lexus. Inside it looks like the flight deck of the Enterprise all white leather and glowing blue dials. Brogue-face is shitting on and on about himself and the company. Colorpure this, Colorpure that. When I was your age and other such shite. How the fuck does he think he knows my age? I have achieved fuck all and I'm telling ya, it aint been easy but how many years has it taken me? For a while, when you were with me Mia, I was almost something. I didn't listen to one word that came out of his shoe mouth. I did fantasise about grabbing the wheel and swerving us into the path of an oncoming truck. "I'm sorry sir, but your son has been in an accident …" You could say I *careered* off the road. Okay, so it's not as good as a *Bluicide* but it would still say, 'Fuck you dad!'

We arrive at a wine bar. Inside was minimalist décor. It was quiet but for a loud shouty group of businessmen, surrounded by a few tables with couples or small groups, glaring at the obnoxious gathering at the bar.

The shouty group were the Colorpure Facilitators. All in matching large collar shirts, some with braces or individual ties to make them at least a bit individual. But it's individual by proxy, as they all have bought the same ties as the top guy. Cloning themselves for acceptance. So, if the individual tie is also worn on the same day as another clone, in the same individual tie, it cancels out the indevidualness.

And then there were the suits. Being adored and gushed at buy the shirts. All talking loud, big hand gestures to draw eyes to fucking huge expensive watches the size of patio tables. Calling each other 'Son'. I understood right there and then, why someone invented the flamethrower. To cull gatherings of stuck up arrogant twats. Shoe face introduced me to the group. "Fellow puritans," he said, 'This is Evans, he's made of the right stuff, working late, a real soldier to the cause." The prick couldn't even remember my wrong name.

"Yo Son, welcome to the Lions club," said one shirt.

"Yahh Son," says another and holds his hand up for me to high five. This is immediately slapped by another from behind. Son? Did he call ME Son? Fuckers younger than me.

"Lions slaughtering lambs bro," the guy behind me shouts, loud enough to blast all the wax from my ears. Shirt number one holds up two fingers to the barwoman. "Duce beeroh's on the tab darl."

24

"What you drive Son?" said the first guy.

I push my way to the bar. "An order on the tab?" testing with a question. The barwoman looks at me and says – "Yeaaah?"

I turn and do a quick head count of the Colorpure wank club. 11 of the fuckers. I turn back to the woman and place an order. "8 unopened bottles of beer, the strongest most expensive you have, a pint of something expensive and two double whiskies." Enough to get me totally wankered.

"So," shouts shirt number 3, "You wanting to make it upstairs then huh?"

"To heaven?" I say sarcastically. But the irony is lost.

"Heaven? Yeah. I like that. Hey guys, the techies call the sales floor heaven!"

Oh for fuck sake.

While waiting for my order, shirt number one approaches me again, "You know why we are called the Lions club?" His face is way too close, spitting on me as he accentuated the 'b' of club. I was going to say something funny, maybe even witty, but this arrogant prick left me no room to answer. "We are the Lions club cos we are lions mate, predators, killers." His fellow shirts, pink faced and glossed with coke and beer sweat, put their arms around his shoulders. "We are hard, cold killers of the sales world. Wild things. Nobody is safe. I could sell any-fucking-thing. Any fucking thing at all." I could sense the overbearing contempt for me, a tech-support nobody, brought to the Lions fucking Den.

Fuck em. I turned and filled my pockets with the bottles

25

of beer, necked one whisky, gulped the pint and grabbed the other whisky. Like I give a flying 747 fuck about what they think. Then the Queen arrives. Marie Claire, slow walking to the bar. Putting on a show, slowly swinging her bag. With all her little bee's around her. Wonder which director she is fucking this week? All the shirts are trying to fuck her. She stops, gives a confused and disgusted look up and down at me, then floats to a stool, made available to her. Five beers and two whiskies in, I'm hanging out to see if I can get a lift home. I have no idea where I am. I'm at the fruit machine and down a few quid. I smell her before I see her, Marie Claire. She drapes herself over the fruit machine. Her breasts eclipse the flashing lights. "So," she said.

"So," I reply. I'm a bit pissed and thought it'd be cool to say the same.

"You a Lion now?"

"Fuck I hope not." Probably not the best answer but it kinda fell out.

"I like you, seen you a few times at work, your funny."

Holy shit. Is she flirting with me? I'm sure she's flirting with me. Maybe she is bored of the manicured and rich and fancies some rough. I bet even if you eat at the finest restaurants you must crave a sneaky Mc D now and again?

She looked me in the eye and said, "I want to know your story, tell me about you."

Well fuck that. What could I possibly say? I am dependant on drugs just to get through the day. I drink so much my

26

back hurts. I steal tampons and try to fuck repulsive women too drunk to say no. Most of the time I don't know where or who I am and the best fitting title for me at work is 'wanker'. No way. Time for the question with a question. "No." I say. Leave a pause for effect "You are the only interesting person in this room. Tell me about you?" Clearly, her favourite topic. Because out came a miss world-esque load of well rehearsed drivel. On and on she went and I'm glazing over.

A beautiful but boring woman wants to fuck me, and I'm pissed. I'm sure she wants to fuck me, all the signals are there, but I'm not sure if my cock would get stage fright. She is so beautiful. Plus I'm not sure if it would be legal for us to fuck as I don't think we are the same species. I can't pass out or bury my face in her shoulder during sex, belch whisky breath, cum instantly, fart loudly then pass out. I need something. I remembered the little pill of speed in my pocket. "Excuse me," I said, "I need to make an important call," and made my way outside. I corner the building and suck in fresh air, swig from a bottle of beer and sink the speed.

From an open window above me, I can hear the 'Team Fuckers'. I must be below the toilets.

"Dude, it's going to be fucking awesome, funny as shit."

"What, what you all laughing at?"

"Dude, doooooooood, MC is going to penguin that cunt Evans."

"Who?"

"C'mon man, keep up, that technical support loser from downstairs."

"No, who is MC?"

"Marie Claire! It's fucking awesome. She hits on some loser like Evans, gets him all frothing and hard. Says she can't wait and wants to suck his cock like right now. Takes him outside, kisses him. She says its so he can taste what he will never have. Tells him to drop his trousers, take off his top. She stands back to get a better look she says then says how good he looks and she wants his cum so calls him over. The topless prick waddles like a penguin cos his trousers are around his ankles and she films it on her phone. Classic or what? Then she emails it around the office and posts it on youtube and her blog, y'know, her 'Penguin diaries' page."

"No way! That's friggin AWESOME," and they all laugh like a pack of Macbeth witches.

I'm not sure what the collective noun is for cunts. A flock? A shoal? A troop? A pod? I call it a *'fuckuss of cunti'*. Not really words, but they are the best I can do.

My blood is boiling. I am savage with rage. Utter, utter, wankers. Nobody is allowed to hate me as much I do. I return to the bar and Marie Claire sashays up to me again. "There you are."

"Here I am," I say and look her in the eye. "Marie Claire, do you have a nut allergy?"

"Pardon?" She seems a little thrown by the question.

"A nut allergy. Do you have one?"

"No," she laughs. "No I don't."

"Good," I say, "Coz I'm going to rub my hairy nuts all over your pretty face."

"WHAT?"

"You fucking heard me you cunt. My nuts, your face. I'm going to give you satchel rash, before I put my balls in your mouth." She is horrified, disgusted. Scared. I don't think anyone has ever spoken to her like that in her whole life and thats just like a heavy foot on a gas pedal for me. I'm on a roll and I want to scare the shit out of the bitch. She goes to walk away. So I grab her arm. "Woah there! Where the fuck do you think your going?"

Embarrassed, she whispers, "You – are – making – a scene," in a robot like fashion.

"Nothing like the crime scene I'm gonna make later. Yeah, you didn't know I'd slipped Rohypnol in your drink did ya? I'm gonna rape the shit out of you in a bit."

"Wh… what?"

Oh shit! Evil is just spewing from my mouth, all the bile, anger and contempt for her, for you Mia, for everyone. Undeserving a victim as she was, I was like a geyser. "Yeah. You know the girl raped down by the football fields, that was me. I'm a rapist and I've been thinking about you for a very long time. Then I see you hear so I think tonight…"

She snatched her arm free and in floods of tears, ran over to the *'Fuckuss of cunti'*. I'm not a rapist, but I am angry and a hateful little man. I remembered the rape from the news headlines. A violent local rape. A horrible thing to say and right there I knew I'd gone too far and tried to suck it back.

Then here they come, the shirts. Angry shirts. Like a fucked up M&S advert.

"What the fuck did you say to MC?"

I ignored them but one of the shirts shoved my shoulder. "I'm talking to you. You can't come into the Lions Club and..."

I turned. All the fury of my shitty life, given a fissure in the rectum so it exploded out like a bleeding turd. "Lions Club? Lions? Look at you. Are you having a laugh? Your not lions, your sheep. Your cattle. Your not free, running the plains and hunting. No, you are cooped up like chickens. Yeah, that's it, chickens. You lot are battery hens in your little cages, clients are brought to you like grain by your masters upstairs and you peck away. With your stupid fucking ties, and stupid fucking shirts. Pecky pecking to produce an egg for your masters upstairs. Your fucking hens. This isn't a Lions club, it's a fucking hen party." I was shouting at this point. And it was at this point one of the shirts punched me in the side of the head.

I was lead to believe it would hurt to get punched, having never been properly hit before. I had quietly dreaded being punched, but, to my delight, it didn't hurt at all.

When I came two I could see stars. Not cartoon stars like Wylie Coyote sees. I mean actual real stars. I woke up outside, looking at the night sky. They had tossed me in

30

the car park. Still, all wasn't lost, I still had one bottle of beer left in my pocket. Anger gave way to resentment and a resigned return to apathy.

I walk into town and trawl the bars, looking for a woman as desperate as me. That will never happen. There will never be a shortage of penis. We don't ration the penis like women do vagina. Even the girl deemed the ugliest in the burns unit can get fucked. If I don't get laid tonight I might go home and try to fuck my toaster. It looks like a double robot vagina. As the night draws on, I slouch in to the seedier bars. The dark clubs on the fringes of the city. Dirty places that offer every kind of stimulation to the lonely, be it chemical, sexual or voyeuristic.

I'm at the bar, looking into my shot of vodka for solutions, when in my peripheral vision, stunning legs brush past. Unstable on my stool, I turn and look. The legs go on forever. Perfect, athletic legs. The tops are hiding in a tiny tartan miniskirt. I watch her walk away, the most amazing back beneath a tight black vest top. She must be a gymnast, or a pole dancer. Long raven blue-black hair to the small of that amazing back. She joined her friends and I couldn't take my eyes off her. She was beautiful. She turned to look at me and smiled. All her friends noticed me transfixed. She gave a cute little laugh and looked again. I did my best 'look shy' and glanced at her. Trying to give the impression of not being a casual sex addict. Truth is I'm a raging fuckaholic that can't get laid. Even if she was sixty years older and liver spotted, with a rotting vagina, I'd still want

31

to empty in it. Well, fuck me, she didn't look horrified. More than that, we were exchanging eye contact. Flirty stares. She is smokin hot and making eyes at me. After a good hour of me bottling it and not talking to her, to my utter shock she starts walking toward me. Second time I've been approached in an evening, so I'm more than a little wary.

"Hi."

"Hi," I say

"Amanda," she says in her sultry voice. She held out her hand. I took it.

"Lovely to meet you Amanda. Your not going to give me a penguin are you?"

"What?"

"Oh, nothing. You look amazing."

"I ammmm amazing hunnnnnnny."

We exchanged pointless, flirty small talk for a while. I was shit at it. Killing the mood with everything I said. It was late, club soon to close and I was about to make my move when she grabbed the back of my head and kissed me. The most violent kiss, it felt like a hovercraft ran over my face. I kinda liked it. Then, she whispered in my ear, "I want to fuck you."

I must have emptied a pint of pre-cum in my pants right there and then. This NEVER happens to me. This, stunning, athletic woman wants to fuck me. I don't have to fool her with the promise of cocaine or the pretence I am a model agent. Me, she wants to fuck ME. It gets better, she takes my hand, walks me passed her friends who all go 'ooOOOOooooohh' and I smile shyly as she leads me away. We thread through dancers and drinkers to the emergency doors. She pushes them open and soon we are in the cool of the night, the full moon highlighting her muscular back as she leads me down an alleyway. Fuck me she was tall, taller than me. She could be from Holland.

We stop at the loading doors of an adjacent club. She slams me against the doors and tries to cave my head in with her tongue. I'm eclipsed in shade, she is painted blue by moon and orange by streetlight, leaving her the colour of Windowline. I am a passenger. She is in control. Dominant. I kinda liked it.

She fumbles with my jeans, unbuttons me. I'm exposed and the chill is erotic. This is crazy. She yanks down my jeans and she follows them to the floor, crouching. Instantly her mouth surrounds my cock, expertly working it. She is slow, deliberate, erotic. I more than kinda liked it. She stands, looks me in the eyes and bites off her false thumb nail, spitting it away. I have no idea what the significance of this is but she is grinning and looking right into my eyes. She did a cute little laugh, so I did a cute little laugh. But as I'm a bit strung out and nervous that I might fuck this up, my cute little laugh sounds like a little girl crying. I immediately try to do a deeper, more manly cute little laugh. This time I sounded like a Wookie. She starts sucking her thumb like a school girl. Full red lips envelope her thumb her eyes locked onto mine. She slides back down, not taking her eyes off me. She has a strange, yet pretty face, with a defined jawline that reminds me of someone but I can't think who. She smells of lavender, juicyfruit and vodka.

She returns her attention to my cock and takes it all in, right up to the hinge. She must have an oral fixation as, by God, she knows what a cock likes. She is making little noises as if my cock tasted of chocolate. Then BAM, she punched her thumb right up my ass. Fuck me, I was so shocked, I went so cross-eyed I think my eyeballs touched. I let out a little scream at a pitch only bats and dolphins could hear as I sank my nails into the wall. So, that explains the nail and wet thumb. She then started thumbing me with such violence, like she was hitch hiking up my ass and sucking my cock with such force, I thought she was going to suck my spine out through the end of my cock and hold it aloft like 'Predator'. She was working me so hard I was sure she would snap my pelvis. It was kinky, yet worrying. I kind liked it but I didn't know if I was going to come so hard I'd blow a hole through her skull or shit in her hand.

She stopped and stood up. Smeared lipstick and a filthy smile. I was open mouthed with shock. And open arsed with damage. This could be the best fuck ever. Filthy bitch.

She then said, with her square jaw, and big head. This Amazonian Goddess, "Lets fuck." I am so happy. Result, score, ding-fucking-dong. She fumbles in her handbag and pulls out a condom. That right there is the international symbol that sex is guaranteed. Put your seat trays in the upright position. Make sure all luggage is securely located in the overhead storage, fasten your seatbelts, Penis will shortly be arriving in Vagina. She looks at me and for a blissful moment, she looks demure and shy. 'Would you like me to put it on?' she says.

"Oh, fuck yeah, roll that fucker on!"

You can imagine my surprise then. Or rather shock, as she pulled up her mini skirt to reveal a rock solid, fat, blue veined cock.

"WHAT THE FUCK?"

She looks at me and instantly there is a mood change on her, I mean, his, face. "Don't act like you didn't know you little cock tease."

"WHAT the FUUUUUUUCK?"

She, I mean, he, then grabbed me by the throat. "Your gonna suck my cock and I'm gonna fuck you, you little shit, leading me on like that."

I was about to shout there was no way that was going to happen but she grabbed me by the hair and slammed my head into the door behind me. My legs go weak. Then she grabbed me by the face, hard. I try to break free and she slaps me. I go to hit her back but have been taught never to hit a woman. Then, she drives her fist into my stomach, goodfella's style and I drop. I reach out to scratch or pinch. I don't know, I'm not much of a fighter. All I do though is pull off her wig and it lands on my head. I look like a bad Ozzy Osborne impersonator. I look up and no way is that a woman I thought. Though his penis was a better clue. Then I realised who she reminded me of, David Coulthard, the F1 driver.

On my knees and I cant breathe, she, I mean, he, is jousting at me with her cock. Its purple shiny dome trying to smash my face in. With each thrust, I am diving my head out of the way. It's epic, like the scene from Starwars where Luke has dropped his lightsabre and Darth is slashing at him with his. Except this is an angry transvestite with an erection. "Suck it," he shouted.

"NO!"

"SUCK IT!" she shouted.

"I will not." I said. Sounding like C3PO.

She kneed me in the jaw. Smashed my head against the door again and I'm almost out cold. She steps back to kick me and lets one go to my gut. Pain like a lightning bolt ravages me. She steps back to deliver a harder kick, but is unsteady on her high heels. Hopping, she unbuckles the strap and removes a shoe, revealing a massive foot. Shit, it might have been her shoe I found in Salcombe. How did I ever confuse this thing for a woman?

With that she stepped back to deliver a mighty kick to my face. I shut my eyes and clenched my teeth, waiting for impact. Waiting for her to do a Jonny Wilkinson on my head and kick my face over the roof. A scraping sound of high heel on tarmac followed by a massive thud and a crashing sound, then silence.

When swinging back to murder-kick me, she's got her hand bag trapped under her foot, lost her balance. And fallen, smashing into a metal wheelie bin and the wall. Like King Kong when he fell off the Empire State building, there she lay. But with a tartan mini skirt on and his cock flopping out. I got up and ran.

I'd like to make a small addendum to what I said earlier about it not hurting when you get hit. It does. A lot. Especially when delivered by an angry transvestite.

## Tuesday.

It's a relief to wake up at home. But I am a mess. In a short time I've gone from never having been in a fight to getting my ass kicked, twice. And one of those by a tranny called Amanda. Oh, I get it, A - Man - Duh. I switch on the kettle, but the light doesn't come on. Even Barbie has gone out. I remember the electric is out. I make my way to the bathroom, piss over the toilet again and catch a glimpse of myself in the mirror. I look fucked up. A mess. I have a swelling on my bottom lip, a big red welt on the side of my head, a graze on my chin and a big dollop of red in the corner of my eye. Like a red biro has leaked. Everything aches. My legs from the walk, the blisters, my liver, my spleen and the various impact traumas to my body. I get my phone to call in sick, but the battery is flat.

I walk to the kitchen and plug it in to charge and call work. Tell them I've died. But it stays blank. I press the on button. Nothing. Oh yeah, the electric is out. So, I start the walk to work with no idea if I'm early or late.

The bus ride there, I draw lots of stares. I look at my

reflection in the window and not only do I look like a crash survivor, I haven't done my hair. Its all jutting up at odd angles right at the back of my head and theres a fag-but stuck to one side. I flick it off and lick my hand. I try to flatten my hair. A woman looks horrified. I look down at my hand, and my mouth was bleeding. I was using blood as hair gel.

I get to work. I should go to reception and find Marie Claire but can't face it. I was way out of line and should apologise, but, right now I just want something warm in me. A coffee and something to eat. I walk under the roller shutter dispatch doors at the rear of the building. It was like being the Fonz. People just stopped what they were doing and looked at me with amazement. Yaaaaay, I thought. I am the guy who spoke like shit to that stuck up bitch Marie Claire, I'm your new hero. Bulldog sees me and runs up to me. "What the fuck are you doing here man?"

"I work here remember."

"Fuck that dude, you can't come in here, they're looking for you."

"Looking for me? Who's looking for me?"

"Police dude, they say you're a rapist."

"What? No, that's just a little misunderstanding dude. I just said that shit to scare Marie Claire."

"What?"

"It was a joke. I'm not a rapist, I'll go sort it out."

"What about the tranny you raped and left in a coma last night dude?"

"WHAT? WHAT THE FUCK?"

The world has just stopped spinning. Bulldog continued, "Yeah, you were on telly this morning dude. You are wanted in connection with the football field rape and for raping a tranny. They gave out your name and even had a photo-fit picture of you and everything. It even looked like you. I mean they never look like the person but this one REALLY looked like you..."

"Well don't sound so fucking pleased they got the fucking picture right dude." I'm in a panic. I want to hyperventilate but my whole body hurts. "I didn't rape anyone dude. The tranny. She attacked me."

"He," said Bulldog.

"What?"

"He. It was a *HE* dude. The tranny was a dude, dude."

"I fucking know that. She fell over. Look at my face. SHE did this." I point at my face.

"He," said Bulldog. " Erm it's okay y'know, your not the first."

"Not the first to what? Be mistaken for a rapist?"

"No, y'know," Bulldog mimed quote marks, "Didn't know she was a he."

"What?"

"All I'm saying is," more quote marks, "I kinda know what it's like."

"What? What the fuck are you talking about dude? And stop miming fucking punctuation."

"Okay, well a few years back dude I went to Thailand

and scored a prostitute that turned out to be a chick with a dick. It was pretty weird."

"Wha... what was pretty weird?"

"You know, that it was a chick with a dick!"

"No, I get that bit," I said, "What was weird? Did you do it?"

"Well, yeah, I'd already paid. It's okay though is what I'm saying, it's only a chick with a dick."

"No dude, it's a man, with," mimed punctuation, " boobs."

Bulldog got defensive. "No, they are chicks with dicks, and stunning too."

"Mate," I say, "It isn't a woman that's had a penis surgically stitched on, its a man that's had a boob job... and you bummed it?"

"Well I'd already paid! She'd cost me 300 Baht. I didn't want to lose that kind of money."

"That's like the price of two beers dude!" I said. We were getting a bit off track. "Anyway, mine tried to rape me." I pointed at my face again. "SHE did this to me."

"HE," said bulldog, nailing his point home.

"Yeah, right. He. He did this. As for the other rape, I know fuck all about it other than what I heard on the news. It was a joke."

"Then go tell the police that. Tell them where you were on the night the girl got raped dude."

Oh fuck. Oh fuckiddy fuck. I have no idea where I am from one night to the next or what I did. Jesus how is that going to sound? FUCK. Oh fuckiddy fukiddy fuck.There is

40

no way they are going to believe me. "Dude," I say, "It wasn't me. Can I crash at your place for a few days till everything calms down?"

"I don't know man. I've got my own problems. You got to know about 'em dude coz their kinda your problems too. Can't you stay with friends?"

"I haven't got any friends. All my friends were Mia's and she won full custody in the split. Please, Bulldog? Just a couple of days, till they work out it wasn't me?"

I kept pressuring. Until Bulldog caved, gave me the address and gave me two rules. Not to open the curtains and not to open the door to anyone. I guess that goes with the territory if you pedal drugs. More walking, to Bulldogs flat. More protests from body. Lucky I look so fucked up, that not even my mother would recognise me.

I arrive at Bulldogs flat. Slide in the key and open the door. The house is in the student quarter of the city. Old, huge Victorian, converted to multiple flats. I walk in and it's surprisingly tidy. I'm jealous. High ceilings, airy. Walls the colour of sand. I realise I have been in the same clothes for near on two weeks. I'm more standing in them than wearing them. Bulldogs place has a washer dryer so I strip, put my clothes on to wash and run a bath. I need to relax, think, and find a way to sort this shit out.

I'm walking about Bulldogs flat, naked. Eating his biscuits and drinking his tea. I feel like I'm violating him and his space. So I look for something to wear. All I can find is a dressing gown that is waaaay too small. Half way up my arms, and only down to the top of my thighs. Like a mini skirt. I pull back the curtains, let in some light. Things look better in daylight and they can't get any worse. It will sort itself out I thought. I go to check the bath and it's filling nicely. Fuck me but even the Dog's bathroom is nice and fucking tidy. It makes me think about sorting my life out. My thought is broken by the chunk from the toaster popping up two golden slices of toast. I wander to the kitchen. Admire the wooden floor. Classy, I thought.

As I turn around, there are two massive guys in leather jackets standing behind me. They are wearing matching leather gloves. Other than on old ladies and racing drivers, leather gloves are never good news. I freeze, mid chew. The first one grabbed me and threw me across the flat. I smashed a small, Japanese looking table as I landed face down. The other grabbed my feet and pulled me back. I thought this was going to tear my bollocks off as he dragged me backwards over the carpet. The little dressing gown was now bunched around my armpits. My recently thumbed ass was on full view. Thug two picks me up, slaps me and pushes me on the sofa. "You naawty boy." The South London accent, hard and sounding like nails dragged down slate. I hold up my hand and point, it's a 'wait one minute' point coz I was choking on the toast. He slapped me again across the face, dislodging the toast and firing it into the window where it splatted and stayed. Thug one picks up a magazine off the side and throws it at me, followed by the plate my toast was on. It frisbiees into my forehead, bounces off. It

42

hurt like a bastard. "We ain't faackn round you little shit, give us what we want aw you will wake up wan mownin, an find yawseef dead!" He had a face like a used shovel, as if someone had magic markered two dots for eyes, that gave him the appearance that he was looking for his own face.

"How can I wake up and find myself dead, surely if I was dead I wouldn't waAAAKE" Thug two steps forward with his hand raised to hit me again. Embarrassingly, I curl up in a ball to hide from the impact. Just like a girl. The bald headed Thug two continued. "Lissaan, fawty eight aaurs, get it to ass in fawty eight aaurs aw you is dead, understaan?"

With that, they left. Could today get any worse? Who the fuck were they? They must have thought I was Bulldog. I grab my phone to call him, but the battery was still dead. I go to plug it in but his charger does not fit mine. No landline I could find. What now? There was nothing I could do. I can't warn Bulldog, not in this dressing gown and with my cloths in the washing machine. Besides, its not like they'll be back. Bulldog must owe them money or gear or something.

Problem: anxiety, fear, panic. Answer: bath. Shame to waste it. I can relax and think what my next move will be. Nothing seems like a good plan right now. Surely these two London guys must think I'm Bulldog? So I'm ok, all I've got to do is warn him. That solves that. Just need to figure out how to solve my rape crisis. I've been beaten up three times, and I'm not fucking liking it. I'm not liking it at all. I slip into the bath. The warm water caresses every inch of my skin. Displacement of my weight in water eases the pains, as if the water is absorbing the aches, ready to drain them down the plug whole. I lay there, exhausted. Every ten minutes or so, toeing the hot tap, topping up the temperature. I could happily lie there for the rest of my life. All the chaos moved further from my mind. I tried to sit up, get a bottle of shampoo by the taps, but my God it hurt like fuck, I couldn't bend. I was sure I was broken in there. So, using my feet, I grab the shampoo and maneuver it too my hands. I grab it. So far, so good. I hover the bottle above my head, invert it, to get a healthy dollop of shampoo to my hair. Nothing comes out. I squeeze and look up. A giant shampoo turd plops right in my fucking eye. Stings like a bastard. Fucking eyeball fire. Total cunt of a day. I slide down, submerge my head, rub my eye and wash my hair. I bask in the sensory deprivation, the silence. I lie under water for a good long time with just my nose sticking out. Loving the solitude. As I surface, I blink a few times. Where the fuck did the policemen come from? The rooms full of the fuckers. Fantastic, this day just gets better. Within seconds, I am returned to the front room and am back in the tiny dressing gown. Hands cuffed behind my back. Policemen busy themselves around the flat, searching high and low. Through the draws, taking the covers off cushions, flipping the sofa, pulling at the carpet. It made a distressing fart noise as it released its grip on the carpet tape. A tall,

44

thin detective, with a thin rodent face and a stoop, in a too obvious trench coat stood next to a shorter detective, also in a too obvious trench coat. The shorter of the two had a face like an unmade bed. 'I am Detective Cuvlum and this is Detective Short of Devon and Cornwall Police. I am arresting you on suspicion of the alleged supply of a controlled substance. You have a right to remain silent.'

As he rattled off my rights, I was wondering what the fuck was going on. Controlled substance? They must think I'm Bulldog. Thank fuck I was only being arrested as a drug dealer and not a rapist. If that makes sense. I sat on the sofa as they went through the place. A female police officer asked me to close my legs. I was naked but for the midget dressing gown, and my lunch was hanging out. Not the tip they were looking for.

After sitting for a good while and fielding shitty glances from policemen and policewomen, I get lead out to a car. The street was a parade of neighbors, none of whom were mine. Another officer, walks to the side of Cuvlum, "Nothing."

So, a fruitless search then, I thought.

# 3

## The Police station. A sore balled virgin.

I sat in the interview room for an eternity. Four chairs bolted to the floor, shiny plastic. They were cold to the touch. This was fantastic, as I alternated between them, resting my hot, enflamed carpet burned balls on them. It offered soothing temporary relief. Swollen, my gonads fell over the plastic like two pink, wet teabags. The hum of the fluorescent light was driving me mad, and once I focused my ears on it, it seemed stupidly loud. I wonder if the cold was to make me uncomfortable. I tried to pull the table closer to sleep on it, but it was bolted to the floor and the gap was to large to span. Designed for discomfort. Hours in, the door opened and in strode the detectives. Cuvlum and Short. Short remained short and standing. Cuvlum sat. Sipped a coffee and looked through a fat manila file, in silence. Post long dramatic pause, designed to unsettle Cuvlum finally broke the silence, "We've been watching you for some time." Clearly a Matrix fan. Cuvlum had a full on plum in his mouth, middle class Oxfordy type plum. You could tell his disheveled clothing was an attempt to fit in amongst his more working class peers. Also, he was clearly full of shit. They had no idea I wasn't who they wanted, so they couldn't have been watching me.

"I'm not who you think I am," I said. I instantly regretted saying this, as saying who I was meant my arrest for rape. If I go along with this charade, I might get released under caution and disappear, for them to discover the real person they are looking for later, I guessed. As they found nothing, this might well be the case.

"Who do you think we think you are?" Cuvlum said.

"I think, you think, you know."

"I think you don't," said Cuvlum.

"You think, I think what you thought. I don't. But I think, you think what you think is what I thought," I said.

There was a long awkward silence. Cuvlum and Short looked at each other, looking confused and lost in the pointless conversation. After a short fluster of the file, he continued. "We didn't find anything at your house. Why don't you make it easy on yourself and tell us where it is?"

"You were just there, you know where it is," I said.

"Know where *what* is?" questioned Cuvlum, trying to catch me out.

"My house," I said.

"What?"

"You said you were at my house and wanted me to tell you where it is. But you were there, so you must know where it is."

47

"Don't try to be clever son," he plummed.

"'Look, Mr. Love-cum," I said, "I just answered your question. You were not being at all clear."

"It's Cuvlum," he said, "Detective. What do you know about J-Lo?"

This threw me. "What?"

"J-Lo, what do you know?"

"Uhh, South American, Cuban I think, had a couple of kids, singer, actress. Her music sucks but she has made some good films. I liked the one where she goes into the mind of a killer and..."

"You think this is funny son?" Cuvlum barked. "You are in it up to your ears sonny Jim."

"Mr. Love-cum," I taunted, "You asked me what I know about J-lo?"

Cuvlum drank from his cup, composed himself, loosened his tie and unbuttoned the top of his shirt. He shuffled the file, turning some pages as he regrouped. He had grown visibly higher on the red scale. I know about red scales, its my job. If interested I'd say he'd gone to Pantone red 7146.

"Jay Lowe." He spelt it out for effect. "J-A-Y L-O-W-E, son of the notorious Rob Lowe."

"Rob Lowe?" I said, "Rob... Lowe? C'mon is this a fucking joke?"

"I don't see the joke." Cuvlum had a dour straight look.

"Rob Lowe, ROB – LOWE?" I say, waiting for a 'Oh yeah'. But getting nothing.

"The Cell," said Detective Short.

"What?" said Cuvlum

"The Film with J-Lo, when she gets in the mind of killers. It was The Cell."

"Look, I know nothing about either Lowe. I have no idea who they are," I said. "Am I under arrest? You have less on me than I have on me so if you are not charging me I want to go home."

"What about Stadnyk?"

"Who?" I slapped my palms down on the table. "Are you going to go through every name in the fucking phone book till I know someone? Because it would be quicker if I told you who the people I know are, like my Nanna and ..."

Cuvlum barked me down again. "Stadnyk. Ukrainian Mafia. Ring any bells? We believe two of his thugs were in your flat. We watched them leave."

Fuck. This was serious. Ukrainian Mafia? Do they think I'm Bulldog? Just then I realised I didn't know the Dog's real name. Was he Jay Lowe? Were the Ukrainians after him? How the fuck did I end up in this mess? I felt like a fucked up Alice in a very shitty wonderland.

"Why were they there? We heard an altercation. Your flat had signs of a physical disturbance. Want to tell us about it?"

"Uh, yeah, we were fighting."

"Why?"

My face looked a mess. I look like I fight a lot so I said the first thing that came to mind. "You know that film, Fight Club, the one with Brad Pitt?"

"Yes," said Cuvlum

"Great film," said Short.

"Well it's a bit like that. We have a club where we beat each other up. We call it a beat off. We get together and beat off."

Cuvlum wrote it down in his file. "Tell me more."

"That it really, a group of guys just get together and beat off. Some times we will go to watch other guys beat off, and then when they are done, they watch us beat off."

Cuvlum wrote more. I said, "I bet you two would look great beating off."

Cuvlum smirked with pride. Then he contemplated the facts. I think he knew he didn't have enough to keep me but to officiate the proceedings he read back from the spanish inquisition.

"You like to beat off?"

"Very much so," I replied. "Us guys meet up, fist each other, then watch each other beat off."

"Fist each other?" Cuvlum seemed perplexed.

"Yeah, we, you know, we erm fist each other."

"I'm not sure I follow." Cuvlum really was was none the wiser.

"You know, fisting. You must have seen it on TV or in films, where rappers or gangsters touch the knuckles of their fists together? Well we call that fisting. You in the establishment shake hands, us in street culture like to fist each other. It shows respect when a guy lets you fist him."

"So you like to fist these gentlemen?"

50

"There is nothing like a good fisting. I mean you've got to know a guy well before you can fist them don't you?"

"I suppose you do. And you say there is an underground club, where guys watch other guys fist each other and beat off?"

"Yep."

"And where does this happen?"

"Oh all over. Guys beat off at home a lot and you can often find guys beating off in public toilets."

"Public toilets?" He said as he finished up his report. The banter continued. I like the police but this was an obvious shake down and they were shaking down the wrong guy. They had no evidence to hold me. Nothing of any substance anyway. No substances at all in fact. They couldn't keep me there, as had they had fuck all to charge me with. I was taken to the desk sergeant after a long and boring 'We'll be watching you' speech.

Standing in the reception bit of the station in a tiny dressing gown, surrounded by families reporting crimes and traffic fine payers I felt a right twat. The desk guy slid a form for me to sign under the perspex safety screen. I was about to fill the sections with utter bollocks when I dropped the pen. I bent to pick it up, showing my whole asshole and dangly scrotum, adorned with a double-testicle weeping carpet wound, to the room full of people. This caused a ruckus. A policeman coming in with a man in cuffs shouted, "Hey you! Your junk sir. Put it away or go back in the cells. Your choice sir." I pulled the front of the mini gown together

51

but this made the back ride higher so I was made to sit and wait for transport which stopped me from filling out the forms. I was like a Ninja in an ill-fitting dressing gown. I will have slipped in and out of that police station without leaving a trace. I sat there, below a poster of my face. I was wanted for rape.

A very strange man, bottle-feeding a plastic baby, winked at me as I waited for my taxi home.

# 4

## Stadnyk.

But I can't go home. Not that I don't want to or that things have got a bit rapey I literally can't go home. My clothes, that with any luck will be dry, keys and phone are all at Bulldogs flat. I want to go home. Everything hurts. I just want to eat, sleep, and I want a strong black coffee, poured over a bed of crushed ketamine. Then I want to do what Sigourney Weaver did in Alien. You know, where they put themselves in a deep sleep through prolonged space travel. Long enough for the police to find the real rapist, find that I'm not a drug dealer and for the drug dealers to work out I'm not Bulldog. Long enough to wake up and it all be over. But that has problems too. It would seem some bad people are after Bulldog and so are the police. I have to warn him, help him sort his shit out. Besides, where else would I get my survival products from? It's not like I know a lot of dealers. Bulldog is the only friend I have, and even though he doesn't consider me a friend back, I have to warn him. And pick up the Ketamine I'd bought. OK, so I'm being selfish, maybe I'm not warning him coz he's a friend, he has my gear and I have nowhere else to get it from. I've often wondered how people with drug problems score when they move town. Drug dealers aren't easy to find. They don't advertise. You never see 'Ketamine Sale' signs, or listing for area drug dealers in your local Gumtree web listing. Maybe drug dealers know what to look for and approach you. Look at me. I look like I've been gang raped by a heard of rhino.

The taxi drops me back to Bulldogs house. The front door is slightly ajar. So being the brave little Ninja that I am, do I kick in the door? Do a roll in to the hall and land in a Ninja karate stance? Nope. I hide behind some bins. I'm there so long that my legs go dead and I can feel myself going sleepy. Proper exhaustion like sleep I mean, not drug sleep. Nothing comes in or goes out of the house. So, after being crouched outside, and pedestrians walking past me shouting things like "Put it away" at my carpet burned genitals hanging on full display, I make my way into the house and into the flat.

Its quiet, except for the hum of the fridge and the distant tick off the wall clock. Still nervous, I stealthily Ninja walk to the washing machine, pop it open and take out my clothes. They are not wet, but their not dry. Everything today is difficult, have you ever tried to quickly put on not dry jeans? Ten minutes of jumping around and I'm out of the door walking home.

The day is almost behind me. I'm freezing thanks to the

damp clothes, and all I need is to get home and get to the cookie jar. My mind is like a fog. I keep running through the events in my head but nothing makes sense. I have to warn Bulldog. These thugs gave me, or rather Bulldog 48 hours to get it too them, but get what? They didn't know who I was and I didn't know who they were. I couldn't even call them if I wanted to. Bit of a pisser really.

Finally I'm back at my flat. I found the key for the meter, walked to my local news agent, where the Indian guy said, "Welcome to my store," with a big beaming smile. This would be nice if was my first visit. But it's not. I've been in this shop probably every other day for the last two and a bit years and he still doesn't recognize me. Fucker. He recognizes other customers, the ones with their pension books. I've made small chat, bought vast amounts of lager and recently the cheapest vodka. And now, right below his nose, on the front page of the fucking local paper is a big picture of me under the headline 'serial rapist' and he still doesn't recognize me. Tosser.

My phone is on charge, the key is in the meter and there is bread in the toaster. I'm trying to think through this situation. The cow cookie jar is looking at me. It's no good, I need to warn Bulldog. Help him to sort his shit out. I power on my phone, and instantly I see a different screen saver. I wait for it to clear. As it does it reveals a picture of thug number one, he's holding up a piece of paper with 48 hrs written on it and a phone number. This sent a chill up my spine. Not only did they have my number, they had now told me how to contact them. I'm in a corner so have to do something. Fucking phone. Typical, it had just enough charge to power up for those bastards to take a picture but earlier it didn't have enough power to tell me the fucking time.

Menu, address, name, bulldog, call number. I wait for him to pick up, but it goes straight to answer phone. I don't leave a message. I send a text 'Need to talk. Urgent. Pick up'. Wait 5 and call again, and he answers "Whose this?"

"You know who this is Bulldog, the name comes up, it's me."

"Yeah. Just a test, I'm at work man what's so urgent?"

"Listen," I say, which is pretty pointless as he is on a phone so all he can really do is listen but I figured it added urgency. "You gotta leave work now. Just go man, you are in real trouble dude."

"What?"

"They are after you dude, I've just been given a right kicking cos of you. Get out now and go. I will meet you at your flat and explain then."

Bulldog's voice dropped to a whisper. "Fuck man. Your kidding?"

"No dude, you gotta go."

"Your kidding?" he said an octave higher.

"No. Go."

There was a long pause. I could tell he was thinking it through. Considering the options. Hatching a plan...

"Your kidding?"

"No Bulldog, No I'm not. Go. Just leave. Now"

"Tell me your kidding."

OK, so maybe expecting such intelligence was a big ask from Bulldog. "No I'm not kidding. Fucking meet me at yours in an hour. Go, just go *NOW*."

I hung up.

I hobble all the way back to Bulldogs flat, for the third time in a day. The only mess in it is mine. Well, not mine but you know what I mean. I straighten things out the best I can then get round to the table. The broken table. I try to fix it but cant. So I try to balance it like a sort of table Jenga but can't. I didn't want Bulldog to come home and find such a distressing mess. I then sit and wait. I turn on the TV but can't find the remote control to take it off stand-by, give up and turn it off again. Wander about the flat, waiting for Bulldog to get home. I make a coffee, and as soon as the hot liquid hits my stomach I'm in pain. My gut is gurgling and twisting. I run to the toilet, shoes and socks off, trousers down. I have a burning sensation as if my guts are acid. I sit on the toilet, I have a desperate feeling I'm going to violently shit. It feels a bit like when a transvestite sticks her thumb up your ass, but all I can do is pee. It's like my guts are twisted. I look into the bowl to check for poo. Nothing. But there's blood in my urine. I'm broken! I sit there and think I might be dying, then the pain abates. I inspect the Ribena in the toilet and have an overbearing sensation of dread.

I return to the front room, lie back on the sofa and try

to chill. I try to shut my eyes and relax, think happy thoughts. I recall the last days events, my conversation with Marie Claire had me chuckling. Once I've sorted this mess out, I will sort my own mess out.

Where the fuck is Bulldog? It has to be way more than an hour. When you factor in the walk, plus the time milling around here, he should be here by now. Where the fuck is he? So I get my phone and call.

"Bulldog."

"Yeah."

"What the fuck man? Where the fuck are you?"

"At home dude, like you said, waiting for you."

"Don't fuck about man, this is serious."

"I'm not fucking about dude, I'm at home, waiting for you."

"Mate," I say, with an angry voice, "You ain't, cos I'm in your flat right now, waiting for you, and there is no sign of you, so where the FUCK are you?"

"Oh... Ooooh." Bulldog sounded like he'd just worked something out.

"What?" I said. I got no reply. "WHAT?" I shouted.

"Dude, are you where I sent you this morning?" Bulldog sounded weary

"Yeah, *your* flat."

"That's not *my* flat dude."

"What? Well who the fuck's flat is this?"

"A guy called the 'Chemist'. He was a student who I bought my gear from. Y'know the shit I sold you, and other stuff. He asked me to feed his cat and water his plants n stuff. He said suddenly he had to go away for a while."

"WHAT! Your fucking shitting me?"

World implodes!

"So the bastards that beat me up think I'm him not you?" I said.

"I don't know. Maybe. Sorry man. Just tell them you are you."

"FUCK."

"Yeah," Bulldog offered.

"The police want you too though," I remembered. "I was arrested and taken to the station, two detectives, must have thought I was this Chemist and not you but they asked what I knew about you. You are in this, you have to help me sort it out dude."

A 'Cuntastrophy' I called it. It's not a word, but it's the best I can do.

Bulldog went on to say your kidding about a thousand times, as he spiraled into another panic attack. I honestly thought a drug dealer would be a bit more calm. With a life of dodgy deals and dodgy friends I thought he would have developed a survival attitude not blind panic. I suggested we both calm down, sleep on it and sort out a plan in the morning. I told Bulldog to call in sick. I had probably been sacked, so there was no pressure on me to call anyone. The plan was simple. Inform baddies I'm the wrong guy. Inform police I'm the wrong guy. Wait for transvestite to come out of coma. Wait for police to catch rapist. Easy. I'm playing the scenarios around in my head as I make the walk home. Again. I'm a wreck, I hurt bad and every now and then I either get spasms of pain or the urgent desire to shit. Sometimes, for variety, both together. But, my ruined guts are blocked. I wondered if I was dying. Would my blue assassin at Colorpure be disappointed if he never got the chance of killing me? Funnily, as often as I'd thought about death, I concluded that, actually I don't actually want to die. So deep in thought was I that I didn't see the limousine slowly rolling alongside me. The window of the long black car wound down, revealing a silver haired gent, with a face the colour of a brick.

"Get in."

"Thanks, but I'm ok walking, it's a lovely day." It was overcast and drizzling and I'm limping and walking with a hunch.

"Get in."

"Honestly, I'm fine thank you." Stabbing shit pain and fear make me move from a hobble into a fast walk. I must look like Quasimodo in a marathon. A very big man gets out of the limousine and blocks my path as the car draws next to me again.

"Meester Stadnyk tolda you to geet in." A Russian sounding accent that perfectly justified my fear.

"Oh, so, you're the Ukrainian Mafia then?" I said.

He draws back his arm and a fist the size of a loaf of bread hit me. For the second time in as many days, all went black.

As is all to often the case I woke up in a strange place. What is worrying though, is that its happening far too many times without my consent. I'm on a big leather couch, in a very plush office. Rococo wallpaper, green leather topped desk. The room looked scary, because for all the luxury, there was not a single personal item, no pictures on the desk or hung on the wall. It was like a theatre set with no point of reference. I have discovered that when petrified, like right now, my brain needs something to hang on to. I can feel rocks of dried blood in my nose and its iron taste in my mouth. I now hurt even more. I sit up and the brick faced Mr. Stadnyk is sat at the desk. He oozes power and authority. Shit a brick. This is fuckin big time serious.

"Good heevening my friend, I trust you rest well?" His kind words clashed with his comedy Ukrainain accent and had an undercurrent of malice.

"No, not really, my face hurts." I look down. My newly washed t-shirt has dried blood on it. "Look," I continued, "I'm not who you think I am."

"Who do you thing I thing you are?" He asked.

Not the 'who' game again? I thought better than to try to piss off a Ukrainian Mafia boss. "The Chemist." I said, working for a reprieve. "You think I'm the Chemist but I'm not."

"Hmm," he pondered, rubbing his chin. "You like Jews?" He said.

Jews? Huh? Why was he asking me about Jews? Are Ukrainians Jews or Muslims? Do they hate Jews? What

61

could I possibly say that wasn't going to get me hurt, killed or both?

Stadnyk was imposing behind his desk. It was then I sensed the shadow. I looked behind and Mr. Huge, the one who hit me in the face, was silently standing century and doing a good job of scaring the shit out of me.

"Jews?" I said.

"Yes, Jews. You like Jews?"

"Uhh, do you like Jews?"

"I do. I do," he nodded.

"Then so do I."

Stadnyk threw me an odd look. Looked over at The Hulk, who shrugged and returned the confused gaze to me.

"So, you like some Jews?"

I couldn't talk my way out of this. I had no idea what the conversation was about. I was lost, so I said, "Look, I don't understand. I honestly have no idea what you mean." Had I been mistaken for a Nazi, an Israeli or what? Am I only meant to like some Jews? Why not all Jews?

"Jews. I have orange Jews, apple Jews, grapefrut Jews, anda carranberry Jews, you don look so good. Thought you might like some Jews."

"Oh!" Relief washed over me, so much so that I felt like I was going to shit myself , but I didn't need to worry about that coz I was broken down there. Knowing my luck I will die from septicemia before I get killed. Death by blood disorder, via an un-laid turd does not say 'Fuck you Dad' like an assassination does.

"JUICE! Oh you said juice."

"This is what I said," he sounded insulted but looked agitated.

"Yes please, some apple juice would be very nice," and it would, if only to soften my stools.

"I'm not the Chemist," I said.

Stadnyk retrieved two glasses and a bottle that was very elaborate and expensive looking and poured two large measures of apple Jews. He passed me one and then leaned on the edge of his desk. He smelt as expensive as the bottle looked.

"I know," he said. "You rapist."

I have to say, this threw me somewhat. This was the first person that didn't mistake me for someone else, even if he did call me a rapist. "So, if you don't think I'm the Chemist, why am I here and why did Mr. Enormous here hit me?"

"He thought you no come. I need talk to you."

"Doesn't he know the word please then?"

"I know you. I own many bar and club and two casino. Have you on CCTV, you have problem, I have problem, we help each other yes?"

This didn't sound good. Not good at all. Why the fuck would a Mafia boss need the help of a nobody like me? However, what choice had I other than to go along with the conversation? "Go on," I said.

"You have two problem, mans who think you are Chemist, and police who think you are rapist yes?"

"Yes."

"I can make both problem go. You like this?"

"Yes." I would love for this guy to solve my problems but cant help feeling that this is a deal with the Devil himself.

"I see you. You filthy dirty boy, like dog. In my clubs. Many night you drunk, try to pick up drunk bitches, you fuck anything if you can, I like that. Many, many times we see you. You like fucking yes."

"I guess."

"The mans who attack you, they did for this." Stadnyk held up a flash drive, then placed it on the side of the desk, looking down at it as if it was a divine gift from the Gods. "You know this is?"

"A flash drive?"

"No, you know what on this?"

"I have no idea." Just like I have no idea where this conversation is going now.

"This is recipe. Not any recipe. Not recipe for cake. This make scentless, tasteless cocaine. So no can detect at customs with dogs, scanner nothing. Nothing. Everyone want. I have."

"Wow," I said.

"Your friend Chemist, sell to me recipe, and then bastard promise also sell to other mans. Chemist gone and mans think he is you."

"Where is the Chemist now?"

"Don know, he gone. But we have recipe so no matter."

The Chemist is gone? That didn't sound good at all. Considering what he had developed, I concluded Stadnyk must have killed him to keep the recipe a secret, before he knew that the Chemist dude had already offered it to some other peeps.

"I don't follow. Why do you need me?"

"You fuck my wife."

"I didn't!" This was a well rehearsed defense mechanism.

"No, my wife, you fuck her for me. You lika fuck. I take care of your problems, the mans. I have CCTV of you in bar when rape happen too. I take care of your problems, you take care of mine."

This didn't seem like a good deal. Well it did, sex for fixes. I imagine some hot, younger, peroxide blonde, gangsters wife wanting emotionless, mechanical sex. I can do emotionless mechanical sex. But there has to be a rub if you know what I mean, there has to be a downside.

"I don't understand, why don't you fuck wife?" I've started copying his accent. I can't help it, I do this. Be it Welsh or even fucking, Jamaican it is an accidental stupid habit. Stadnyk gulped at the apple 'Jews' and topped it up with vodka. What happened next seemed pantomimey, but I had no option but to go along.

"Wife and me no longer like." Stadnyk took a slow deliberate mouthful of his drink and continued.

"Tell me, you like horse?" He said, looking into his vodka.

Once again I'm thrown. Horse? Did he say horse? "What?" I said.

"Horse, you like horse?"

"I don't know," I said.

Stadnyk got animated, as if impatient at my stupidity. "How you not know, you either like horse or you don't like horse." His anger flared and would have scared the shit out of me but I was still broken.

"I like horse," I said as I tried to bring the tempo back to calm. "I like horse." I said again, regretting that I am still copying his accent.

"I love horse. In my country, you not man till you fuck horse. You fuck horse?"

Fuck a horse? Is he kidding me? I've done a lot of many filthy dirty things and OK, I admit it, I kinda liked it when the tranny had her thumb up my arse, but fuck a horse? I draw the line at animals!

"Have I? No," I said, trying to not to rile the guy.

"Oh, you should. Best fucks are with horse. But my wife no like I do this. I understand. I have many horse. You know I have horse?"

"No," I said, while hiding the fact I'm freaking out.

"Yes, I have book of all my horse. Boy, Girl, I fuck all. Different colour, different size even, how do you say meed-jeet?"

Oh God. "Yes, midget." He fucks miniature ponies. I suppose it doesn't matter the sex of the fucking thing. I can't imagine anyone who is prepared to fuck an animal would go 'Ewwwww not a male one, I'm not Gay!'

"But we call them miniature." I said trying to stay on the level.

66

"Oh?" Said Stadnyk, nodding in understanding. "Meen-a-ture," he tried.

"Meen-a-ture," said Goliath behind me.

Stadnyk continued. "You like to see pictures?"

"No, I'm fine, really."

"You must, I inseest." With that he threw a large folder onto my lap, I flinched as it landed, the reaction sent a chain reaction of painful spasms from all the beatings. Reluctantly, I looked down at the folder, expecting to see Stadnyk, balls deep in horses and meen-a-ture ponies. I was surprised and kind pleased to find a catalogue of pretty woman. There was an index of race, size and stuff then and at the back, 'Men'. Did he say he fucked ALL of them? Even the guys? I flicked through. Each had a porn name, such as Candy or Angel and a list of likes and what they'd do. "Ohhh," I said "Whores!"

"This what I said." Stadnyk looked annoyed again. "What you think I say?"

Panic...

"Oh, nothing. They are nice. There are many I'd love to fuck here. Quality horse," I said.

"Quality horse," said Stadnyk, nodding.

I tried to compose myself and tried to cross my legs, but all I did was rub the carpet burns on my testicles together. My eyes shrink-wrap in tears but I try to conceal it.

"My wife and I no good. You do fuck on her, I help you."

"You want me to fuck your wife?"

"This is right. Make her happy, make me happy. Make me happy, I make you happy, yes?"

67

It didn't sound like too bad a deal. "Okay."

"She will like you, very kinky is wife."

I thought, this isn't so bad at all.

"When do you want me to do this? When you want me fuck wife?"

"Tonight, and one night a week. You do good you can use my horse. I look after you."

"Why me? Why not a man from your book?"

"You real guy, she will like you. I will explain more tomorrow. I will bring you here again to explain to you tomorrow. You fuck her now. Tonight."

Things were looking up. I'd caught a break. My fruitless pursuit of emotionless sex had potentially landed me the role of 'pointless sex vendor.' It even started to make sense in my fucked up head but if I'm honest, which doesn't happen that often, I was making the facts fit the situation. His wife wants sex, he uses whores, she wants a male one. All the guys in the book are handsome and buff. He doesn't want his hot wife to fall in love with one, so sends over an ugly fuck. Me. Makes perfect sense.

Stadnyk provided me with an address and his Limousine dropped me home. I had a few of hours to kill till my 'fuck-work' so I grabbed some sleep and showered. To fight the pain, I quartered a ketamine tablet. For once I wanted it to do what it was originally intended to do and anaesthetize my aches and pains. 'Fuck-work.' I kept saying it over and over in my head. It sounded amazing.

I wanted to go back to the wine bar, to where the

Colorpure shitbags were and engage them in a conversation.

"Oh, me? I quit my Micky Mouse job. I'm in the sex trade now," I'd say with pride.

"Oh, doing what?" They would ask.

"Me? Oh I'm a fuck-work vendor, I do fucks for fee's baby."

In this I imagine I'm dressed pimpish.

I arrive at the entrance of a posh complex of flats. This was it. Guaranteed sex. I had arranged to meet Bulldog after. I had called him, and, overdoing the drama, made it sound like it was a big deal, that it was all my idea and that I'd made huuuuuuge sacrifices to save his ass. I told him to meet me in the Red Lion pub at nine.

"Your kidding," he said.


The outside of the apartment complex was spectacular, all mirrored glass, natural wood and stainless steel. I press the buzzer to flat 8C and after a slight pause, a crackly voice responded "Hello."

I couldn't work out if it sounded hot.

"Hello, I'm your, uh, visitor," I said, deepening my voice to sound all sexy.

There was a further buzz and a clack as the door unlocked. I pushed through into the foyer. There was a trace citrus sent. I wandered to the lift, selected the penthouse and waited for my short trip to end. Even penthouse had a ring of sex about it. The walls of the lift had a gold mirrored effect, that gave me a temporary golden tan. Aside from the yellow eyes, it suited my new role as 'fuck-work vendor.'

The elevator (it was too posh to be called a lift) stopped at the top floor and the doors opened. There was only one door. 8C, home of Mafia Wife. Destination sex. I was a mix of nerves, excitement and a little bit of dread.

I knock on the door and from inside she shouts, "It's open, come inside." I'd love too come inside, and over your Mafia Wife tits, I thought.

I look about the beautifully decorated flat but see no one. Then I look down a bit. And there she is. In a wheelchair. In a fucking wheelchair. Inside my head I was screaming *"Aaaaaaaarghhhhhhhhhh, Aaaaaaaarghhhhhhhhhh, Aaaaaaaarghhhhhhhhhh."* It was on a loop in my head like a silent car alarm. She had to be late fifties, a big head, covered in scars. She looked like the woman Arnie was inside in 'Total Recall'. Two chins too many. Arms like Pop-Eye, I guessed from hauling herself about in the chair. OK, I'm far from hot. After all the beatings, I look like a bruised banana, but fuck me, she was a whole other kind of mess. She had a big upper body with folds and folds of fat. Stretched over her was a fishnet stocking teddy top, and her tits were kinda shoe-horned in so they fell at different angles. When she moved they jiggled about like a wet gym sock with a baked potato in the bottom. Her thin muscle wasted legs ended in red stilettoed shoes on feet that fell awkwardly like a broken dolls. She looked like Mr. Incredible dressed for the Rocky Horror Show. You wouldn't so much

70

call her fat as lumpy. It looked like she'd just been dragged from a fucking swamp.

"Hi, lets do this, show me what you got big boy," she said. Then smiled. She had to much red lipstick on her lips and her teeth. Thank God I couldn't shit any more. I was about to say, "I'm here to read your meter," when she turned and rolled off away toward the bedroom.

"Your in a wheelchair," I said.

"I know," she replied.

"But. But aren't you paralysed, you know... down there?"

She rolled into the bedroom. There was no way I was going to get a hard cock. No fucking way.

The bedroom was decorated with thick velvet curtains pulled closed. Low lighting and incense slightly masked the stench of cigarettes and antiseptic. She lifted herself out of the chair and did a kind of power-bench press, throwing herself onto the bed. I wished I had her bulging biceps. I'd never lose another fight again. Her landing on the bed wasn't very elegant or lady-like, she crashed sideways, then with her body builder arms hoisted herself to sit up on the edge of the bed. It looked like when R2D2 gets knocked down and gets back up again. She crossed her legs with her hands. They flapped around like over cooked asparagus. It reminded me of how a ventriloquist does it. This would be one fuck ugly puppet, that would make kids piss the bed with fear.

"Spinal. Legs don't do shit, but still have some feeling left in my cunt."

OH. MY. GOD. Did she just say cunt? Did she just call her cunt a cunt? No woman calls her vagina a cunt. I have a little bit of sick in my mouth.

"Besides," she continued, "I still like to *feel* like a woman. And even us disabled women need a bit of cock from time to time." She leaned over, and pulled out a cigarette and a lighter from her bedside table which was topped with loads of empty wine glasses. She struck the lighter three times. It sparked to life on the fourth and she lit the cigarette, it glowed as she drew long and hard on it.

"C'mon, lets fuck," she said out of the side of her mouth, lips holding the cigarette in place one eye squinting through the smoke. This was nothing like Helena Bonham Carter's Marla in Fight Club. She bounced herself further to the edge of the bed, comedy legs swinging about at all angles. She lay back and snapped open the poppers at the bottom of her teddy, revealing her genitals. I say genitals, as I have no other way to describe the mess before me. It was like nothing I'd ever seen. So much red hair and flesh. It looked like someone had run over an orang-utan, then hit it with an axe. Hair on her thighs, ass cheeks, everywhere. And thick, industrial lips, like pickled cow tongues.

"Eat me!" she said. It was clear my life depended on this. I had no choice. I could run out of here and into bigger problems or just block it out of my mind. Man up, I thought. I had do this. I knelt between the asparagus legs and in front of the fleshy coconut and moved my mouth closer to the clump that was her snatch. I pulled her lips apart, it was like I was pulling apart a toasted cheese sandwich. It did a kind of whispering burp, firing a gone off bacon scent to the back of my throat. I sicked a little into my mouth (again). I couldn't. I just couldn't. There was no way my mouth was going on that. It smelt like rotting onions. I looked up, she was on her back smoking. So I got my elbow and kneaded the fleshy clump like I was making bread.

"Mmmmm," she said. "That's good."

Like the fuck you know I thought, as I elbowed her some more. I made some eating noises with my mouth as I carried on elbowing.

"Stick it in me, fuck me hard," she said.

Fuck that, no way was my first thought. Quickly followed by 'will my elbow fit in there?' It looked like one of those 'face huggers' from Alien.

I saw smoke spiralling up from beyond the lumpy netting. I looked around, searching for something I could use, something I could fuck her with. There was no way I could get hard and fuck her. Desperately I looked about for something vaguely penis sized, not that it really mattered, you could probably fit a wardrobe in there. But there was nothing. And then I saw it, on the side by the table, a portable phone. I knelt up as a distraction and said, "You like that?"

"Mmmmm," she said. I slowly reached out. My finger tips were at the phone, I reached. Reached again and it was in my grasp.

"Fuck me now," she said again.

73

I looked at the mess that was her vagina. Then at the phone, back at her vagina, then at the phone again. I couldn't fuck her if I wanted to, my cock was in a worse state than her legs. Without thinking – I stabbed the phone in her.

"I feel it, I feel it. Harder!" she moaned. "Fuck me harder!" So I Tyson punched it in her. I was thrusting my body up and down so she could see me move, in a fake fucking motion, as I sawed away at her snatch with her telephone. Please don't ring I kept thinking. I mashed away at her with the phone for a good few minutes, which I thought was a reasonable fucking period. Then slowed down, kinda wimpered and sawed slower to give the impression that I'd cum. I slid the telephone out. It looked like I'd been spreading mayonnaise with it.

I'd hit an all-time new low. Brings a whole new meaning to phone sex I thought. But it might just have saved my life. "Go. Leave me now," she said.

And I did. Bloody quickly.

I was actually walking slower from the shame, from the emotional damage, than from the physical beatings. I was like a zombie. I'd shut down parts of my brain to deal with the trauma of asparagus legs and I don't think I will ever be able to re-boot those parts for fear of all the detail flooding back. The smell alone means I will never be able to eat hotdogs with onions again, ever. If I couldn't shit before, there was no way I'd ever be able to shit ever again. How is it every decision I'm taking is making things worse?

I get to the Red Lion pub. Bulldog is there with a beaming problem solved smile, but on seeing me, his colour drained. "Dude?" he said.

"Dude," I replied. Sounding hollow.

"Dude?" he said again. "What happened? You look like shit man."

I looked down at his pint and crisps. "The horror," I said. "Oh, the horror." I hover in the awkward silence.

Bulldog looked at me for a while, and finally spoke. "Jeez dude, you want to talk about it?"

"Hang on man, I need a beer first." I hobbled over to the bar, wondering what would best heal my broken body and mind and how to explain to the Dog that I've just phone fucked a cripple.

"Hey," said the barman, "You look just like that rapist guy, the one on the telly."

"Thanks," I replied. Then ordered a Guinness, as its got iron in it, which I figured would help. "And a big bag of crisps. Any flavour except Cheese and Onion." Just saying the words made me think of a vagina that looked like the owners guts were about to fall out through it. The barman told me to go sit, he'd bring the pint over when it had settled. I took my crisps, ready salted, back to the table.

Bulldog was looking at me expectantly. I sat. "Your friend, the Chemist had developed a scentless, tasteless cocaine that can't be detected at customs by dogs and stuff."

"Your kidding?" said Bulldog.

"No, and the police think your him, so until this is sorted, you have to lay low."

"Your kidding. How do you know they want me?"

"Dude, this Detective Cuvlum asked about you by name."

"Your kidding."

"No, I'm not. Your friend the Chemist was double dealing. He sold the secret cocaine recipe to the Ukrainian Mafia, and to these nut jobs from London who beat me up. The Ukrainian's have it and the Londoners want it. I'm guessing the Londoners don't know that the Ukrainians have it."

Bulldog slowly nods, then looks up and then says, "You've lost me."

"At which part?"

Bulldog rubbed the back of his shaved head. "Well, pretty much all of it mate."

"What the fuck! This is serious man, weren't you listening?" My raised voice drew attention from other customers in the bar. "I can't have you tweaked out here Bulldog, you have to straighten up man, this is for fucking real."

"You were going on about Ukrainians and Londoner's. Its confusing."

"Ok. Your friend the Chemist, developed the cocaine and sold the recipe to the Ukrainian Mafia. Got that?"

"Yep."

"The Chemist also sold it to the London guys but seems not to have given them the formula yet . These are the guys who beat me up in what I thought was your flat. Follow so far?"

"Yep," Bulldog nodded.

"Okay, so the Ukrainians HAVE the recipe AND know about the guys from London. The guys from London DON'T know about the Ukrainians."

"Okay, I gotcha now," Bulldog nodded again.

"OK so the two guys from London think I'm the Chemist, who sold them the recipe and say they are going to kill me, which probably means us, if I don't get it too them."

Bulldog looked confused. "Get what to them dude?"

"Wha... the fucking cocaine recipe dude, the scentless cocaine."

"Oh, shit."

With that, a pretty girl approached from the bar, holding a pint of Guinness. "Oh my GOD," she said. "You look just like that rapist guy on the telly."

"I know," I replied.

"Can I get a picture with you?" she smiled.

"What, coz I look like a celebrity rapist look-alike?"

"Honestly, well, yeah," she replied. Before I could protest further, she had already handed her phone to Bulldog to take the shot. She knealt beside me, put her arm around me and smiled. Bulldog framed the picture, "And say rape."

"Rape!" she yelled as he took the shot. I was about to politely ask her to leave but Bulldog butted in.

"Another one looking frightened, and, say rape."

"RAPE!" she yelled, face painted with fear. Bulldog handed her the phone, she thanked me and went back to the bar

"So much for low key you fucking idiot," I whispered.

"You said nothing about low key," Bulldog stropped back.

"In case you have forgotten, I actually AM wanted for rape. I AM the guy on the fucking telly."

"Point taken." Bulldog collected himself, "No more pictures dude. No more pictures."

I continued, "Stadnyk, the Ukrainian Mafia guy is one scary mutherfucker, more scary than the two thugs that beat the shit out of me. He said he will take care of the thugs and the rape thing if I fuck his wife."

"But he knows your not the Chemist."

"I know."

"So, why wouldn't he just let the two thugs kill you so that nobody else knows about the recipe."

"What?"

"Dude, think about it. He thinks you knew the Chemist, and maybe that the other guys were after the recipe. So he probably wanted to know if you knew of the recipe or if it was you who had sold it to them, not the Chemist. Either way, if the two London thug dudes don't get the recipe they take you out and they are tying up his loose ends for him. All he'll need to do is find another dude to fuck his wife." Bulldog looked pleased.

"What, I don't understand?"

"The two guys, the thuggy London dudes, they think *YOU* are the Chemist dude."

"Yeah."

"So, if they kill you, their hunt for the recipe ends coz they don't know that this Stadnyk guy has it. So why would this Stadnyk dude stop them? If I were him, I'd throw you off the sent and let the two thugs get to work and kill you."

"FUCK – your right. We have to get that recipe to the thugs."

"WE?" said bulldog

"*YEAH* we. After me, it's pretty damn obvious that you will be next. Remember, the thugs think I am you. What happens when they discover you are you and I am not you? Besides the police think *YOU* are the Chemist! We have to get the recipe or we're both fucking dead."

"You've lost me again dude."

"Look," I said. "We have to get this mess straightened out or we are both dead. Is that clear enough?"

"Perfectly," said Bulldog.

Bulldog and I start to plan. The plan of plans. To foil everyone and bring about our salvation. We had 36 hours left on the clock with the London thugs. They wanted the recipe and I knew where it was. In Stadnyk's office. The main problem with that was that I'm not sure where Stadnyk's office is. I'd been smashed in the face and taken there and then didn't pay a whole lot of attention on the way out. But Stadnyk said he will see me again tomorrow.

'Rrrrrrrrruuuughhhhhhhhhhh.' My stomach made a deep and loud announcement that I was ruined inside. Bulldog looked at me with shock.

"What the fuck was that dude?" He shot a disturbed look at my guts.

I felt like I'd swallowed a drawer of sharp knives, and I

79

had a terrible urge to shit. I looked at Bulldog, said nothing and then sprinted to the toilet undoing my jeans as I ran across the bar. I kicked open the door of the toilet, took off my shoes and sat on the bowl for what seemed hours. Cold sweat poured off me while I surfed waves of pain caused by the desperate need to shit playing havoc on my traumatised body. It was exhausting. I had to take my shoes off to shit then put them back on, only to quickly take them off again when the urgent sensation to shit came back. But I still couldn't shit. I'd look between my legs into an empty bowl.

I seized the opportunity to wash my elbow free of Mafia Wife 'Jews' before I returned to the table. Bulldog looked at me with concern, "You OK dude?"

"Yeah, it's nothing," I said. "I think I might be hungry." Maybe the Guinness was working. Healing my broken insides I hoped. I went to the bar and ordered more drinks and crisps. "Sure thing rapist ... I'll bring em over" said the bar man.

At the table our plotting continued. "Do you have a car?" I asked.

"Yeah, have a people carrier thing," Bulldog replied, still looking at my guts.

"Good. I'm due to see Stadnyk tomorrow. You follow me, cause a distraction while I'm there and I'll swipe the recipe from Stadnyk's desk."

"What kind of distraction?"

"I don't know, think of something. Set off a fire alarm or something. You'll just have to improvise

80

dude," I said. My stomach said something like 'GuuuurrrRRRRRRRRAAAAAAAAAAAGGGGGGGgggggggghhh.'

Bent double, I ran off to the toilet again, for more pain and phantom shitting. A good half hour later, I return to the table, only to instantly sprint off again to the still warm toilet seat.

Finally I sit back down with the Dog. I have one empty glass and one full glass of warm Guinness. Bulldog has plenty of empty glasses.

Bulldog shot me another look of concern. "Dude, what the hell is wrong with your guts man?"

"Not sure," I said. "I might be dying. I think I've taken one kicking too many and I'm broken inside. It feels like I'm sloshing about in there Like all the kicking's have turned my organs into a stew. I can't eat and I can't shit. I'm in fucking agony."

"I've something that might help you with that," Bulldog offered.

"My Ketamine?"

"Nope." Bulldog rummaged around in his DJ bag and withdrew a packet of prescription drugs. "These."

He placed the box on the table. I picked it up for an inspection. The name read 'Naloxone Hydrochloride 2mg' The box hadn't been opened.

"What the fuck's this?" I asked.

"Gut drugs dude. I had gastric enteritis, really fuckin bad a while back. Thought it would kill me. These sorted it. Took the first box and it cleared it right up. Got this packet left over."

I slid a strip of the blister packed pills out of the box and popped out a whole side, making a tiny beach of pills on the table. "Whoa," Bulldog said, "You can't take that many."

"Fuck it," I replied "I'm taking em. If these don't kill me, London thugs, Ukrainian Mafia, internal injuries or the fucking hole in my guts that the transvestite made with her thumb will. I'd be happy to die without pain right now."

"Thumb?"

"Oh nothing, the transvestite had her thumb up my ass before she tried to rape me."

"Before?" Bulldog was fishing, but it wasn't a tail I wanted to recount.

"She stuck her thumb up my ass. What of it?"

"His thumb," Bulldog corrected.

"What?"

"His thumb. You keep saying she but it's a he. It was a dude who had *HIS* thumb in your ass dude."

"Alright, alright, I know dude, I fuckin know. Just keep your fuckin voice down will ya?"

I swept up the handful of pills, threw them into my mouth and gulped them down with my warm Guinness.

So, a plan was hatched. Throw off Stadnyk by doing his bidding, but before I have to re-fuck asparagus legs. Steal the flash drive with the recipe, get copy of contents of flash drive to police and thugs. Inform police that I am on CCTV in one of Stadnyk's clubs and that I am not a rapist. What could be simpler? After all, it's well known the best plans are formed in pubs. I suggested we both sleep on the plan.

Let it marinate. See if we can make the sponge of a plan watertight. I couldn't go home to my flat coz it was still a bit rapey out there. So I decide to stay at the Chemists. Anyway, this is where Stadnyk thinks I live. That and the fact it was cleaner than my shit hole of a flat. I asked Bulldog for some gear to help me through but he had nothing. Only the stomach pills. I would have to do this sober, and that was never a good idea for me.

I couldn't sleep at all. I had nothing to numb my brain or kill the pain. All I had was the Naloxone. And that felt like it was turning my insides to soup, so the shit would just pour out of my ass. I kept thinking about the mess I was in and the mess I'd be in when the drugs worked. Would I be able to take my shoes off in time? And then I thought about the post mess fallout if I lived through this madness. Mind you, being murdered by the Ukrainian Mafia would make a splendid 'Fuck you Dad'. If I'm not murdered by Stadnyk or the other guys and get through this shit then I will just have the nightmare of trying to repair the rape issues. But then again since I've probably been sacked and then will most likely lose my flat, I'll have to find somewhere to rent. Adverts for flats I've seen say no DSS so it looks like my future is to be a homeless bum. If I'm not dead, I'll need to find an advert that says, 'Flat. DSS and rapists welcome'.

I lied in the dark and couldn't sleep. I thought about having a bath but last time I had a bath in this place, things didn't go so well. I picked at my blistered feet, tearing off the flaps of skin from the burst blisters. No matter how I positioned myself I felt every bruise on my body. I was turning a yellowish green. I'm good at color, it is or maybe was, my job. Can't name this one though. The burst vessel in my eye is going orange. I know that color; Pantone 158. I looked like shit. It was then I realised I hadn't given you a single thought Mia. Not a one. So, my advice to anyone wanting to get over heart break, is to become a cripple fucker rapist, with the looming violent death by London gangsters or the Ukrainian mafia hanging over you. Then I thought about the newspaper and television with me wanted as a rapist. I'm not sure, but I have a strong feeling that it might not help any future plans to get back with Mia or to have a relationship with any another women.

I still couldn't sleep. So I decided to have a wank. I still couldn't find the remote control to find anything on the telly to wank at, or a single magazine in the flat to wank over. So I had to wank a cappella and go without visual aids. But I couldn't get an erection. Maybe my cock was broken too? The thought of having a broken cock was too much and I started to sob. Then I began to cry. I found out two things by doing this. You can't cry your self to sleep. It's too noisy and takes effort. Next time I hear a woman say, "I cried myself to sleep," I will shout, "That right there, is fucking bullshit." Also, I discovered that crying does not make you feel better. I felt exactly the same, but with a wet face. So I sat, slipping in and out of little sleeps, trying to decipher the mess I was in.

# 5

## Wednesday. Grand theft and a bit of auto.

Morning came slowly. I woke about every hour and saw the view outside the window transform from darker shades of blue, through to purples, pinks to orange then finally daylight. I wondered how long I'd need to sit here waiting for Stadnyk to come for me. I called Bulldog at 10am and told him to park at the bottom of the street, wait for Stadnyk, and then follow us. I also told him to take note of where the Ukrainian took me in case he needed to call the police and reminded him to cause a distraction so I could swipe the flash drive. I rehearsed it in my head. The desk where Stadnyk placed the drive, the layout of the office. Anxiety is more exhausting than I thought and I soon slipped into a deep sleep.

A volcano like eruption in my bowls and cramping pain ripped me from my sleep. I was having Braxton Hicks contractions. I was in labour. The Naloxone had worked. I sprinted to the toilet. Off with my shoes, down with my trousers and there I sat. Nothing happened. I still couldn't shit. Nothing but a little blood coloured urine and a trickle of bum-gravy. I remained on the toilet, hoping gravity would assist me. I even considered getting a spoon and trying to scoop the shit out. I had no idea of the time or how long I had been asleep, but I felt very drowsy. More sharp pain and still no shit. The Naloxone hadn't fucking worked after all. I went back to the living room still feeling drowsy. I dug out a large gob of dried snot from the corner of my eye. It was only then that I noticed that the room seemed darker. Mr. Enormous, Stadnyk's goon was standing in front of the window. "Standyk see you now." I checked my phone, it was mid day or should that be hi noon? Time was quickly evaporating. Once again I was in a Limousine. But this time I made sure I searched out landmarks and took account of where I was going in case I needed to call the police.

The long black car pushed through the town traffic like a shark, constantly moving and we came out the other side of the city with no obvious changes in direction. I concluded that they had no idea that Bulldog was following us. I felt nervous and wondered what kind of distraction he would cause. Soon we were gliding through club land. Litter and other evidence of the carnage the night before was strewn about the pavements and doorways. We turned at a taxi rank and a small roundabout. It was an area I knew well from my evenings spent getting told to 'fuck off' by attractive women. I knew exactly where I was.

We rolled up to the access doors of a lock up type unit

set into a wall of other business storage solutions. One side was the distribution area for a Chinese super market and the other was a second hand furniture depot. I tried to have a quick scan of the area but was shoved toward the open door just as I registered that this place faced the back of a couple of nightclubs. I was pushed up the stairs flanked at the front and rear by two of Stadnyk's men. Adrenalin corsed my veins and I started to tremble. I couldn't help wondering if this was my last day on earth. I was fucking scared. The fear and the Naloxone was having some effect as every step I took on the stairs, I let out a tiny little fart. I had a leaky valve and was strafing the guy behind me with ass gas.

Stadnyk was behind his desk, still looking like a gold chained brick with silver hair. Everything was the same. I was shown to the same leather sofa. The air was thick with the same fear and cologne. Stadnyk was looking over something on his computer monitor, I could see the bright magenta's and yellows reflected in his glasses. I thank Colorpure for teaching me the color names.

I could imagine being a Police specialist. "What kind of red was it?" The police would say. "Pantone 485," I would reply. "Damn it, don't be so technical. I need it in process colours goddamn it!"

"Okay," I'd shout. Helicopters would fly overhead and I would continue, "100% magenta and 100% yellow!"

Stadnyk snapped me from my daydream. "My wife like you fuck her."

"Oh?"

"She say you good fuck. This is good. Is very good newsss."

Typical. The only person EVER to complement my sexual technique is a grotesque cripple with whom I'd held my breath and avoided as much body contact as I could while I violently fucked her with a cordless telephone. The ONLY time someone has been kind about my performance and my cock had nothing to do with it.

"She know you, recognise you as rapist."

"She didn't say anything."

"She like this, think it kinky. She has fantasy. You rape her."

"She wants me to *rape* her? Next week – she wants to be *raped*?"

"No, tonight you rape tonight."

"But, that wasn't our deal!" I said. Stadnyk looked at me, removed his glasses and frowned. The look quite plainly said, *'Or I could just kill you now.'* So I continued, "But tonight's good. I can do tonight. But erm I'm not a rapist," I said.

"You are now. Now, you rapist." He laughed.

I had to kill some time. Wait for the Bulldog distraction. "Can I use your toilet?" I said.

"No," Stadnyk said bluntly. Then he continued, "Don't worry, she have fantasy. Important you do exactly as told yes?"

"Okay."

"She have nurse who visit. She do her medication, check her bed sores yes?"

"Yeah, I get it, she has a nurse." Bed sores? Yummy! It just keeps getting better!

"Nurse will put her into sedation, knock her out yes. You turn up at time told. Rape her, then leave."

"Wha... then how will she know I've been there?"

"She watch," he replied.

"Watch?" I said.

"Yes, video in room. You must, er, how you say, *ee-jac-ulate* in her. Fantasy is to wake and discover you were in her. She watch video and then see she has been raped. This her dream. I want her have her dream."

Video? Oh my GOD... has she seen me phone fucking her? I actually HAVE to fuck her. I need to get the flash drive quick as fucking asparagus legs is a fate worse than death. I made a play for time again. "Can I have a drink? "

"No."

Try again. "I really need to pee," I said. "Please, can I use your toilet?"

"No."

Where was Bulldog with his fucking distraction? I had to keep padding. "You wouldn't like it if I pissed on your sofa would you?"

"You do, I kill you. Blood, piss – same to clean up."

C'mon Bulldog! Where are you?

"7.30 tonight you turn up, fuck wife and you leave. Have clothes for you to wear. Here." Stadnyk tossed me a zipper bag. I took out the contents to find black cargo jeans, a black long sleeve t-shirt and a balaclava. A pre-packed rape kit, handy. "Uri, show rapist the door."

With that, Mr. Enormous grabbed my collar, man handled me down the stairs and threw me out the door. It started to drizzle. I have a rape kit. I have no flash drive containing the recipe and it looks like I have to actually fuck asparagus legs for real. It might be better and less painful to kill myself now. Mother fucking fuckety fuck. Not one fucking thing has gone right. I stood there a while, looking up at the sky as the rain pelted my face.

A *catastrofucky* I called it. It isn't a word, but its the best I can do.

I wandered around to the front of one of the clubs. It was called 'The R's' I hadn't noticed the name before. I had never been in club land during the daytime. At night the darkness and neon lights camouflage the decay. Everything looked tired and tatty. The clubs looked like ruins, with flaking paint and smashed windows covered up with wooden panels. I fitted right in, they looked like how I felt. I called Bulldog. "Where the FUCK were you dude?"

"I lost em dude," he said.

"How? How do you lose a massive, black Limousine? HOW?" I demanded.

"When I stopped for petrol," he said. "I lost you."

"You cunt!" I shouted, "You absolute, total cunt. What the fuck did you stop for petrol for?"

"Duhh," he said. "I'd have run out else."

"Run out? RUN OUT? You fucking idiot – you get the fucking petrol before you start the fucking following bit - You utter cunt!"

"I didn't think, okay," he said.

"No, it's not fuckin okay, you fucked everything up. One thing. You had only one fucking thing to do. Follow us and cause a fucking distraction."

"Thats two things." Bulldog said, all stroppy. "Maybe I'll say fuck it and let you sort your own shit out dude!"

"Because, if you do that your dead," I replied. "I don't have the flash drive, I can't save my ass and so I can't save yours either. AND, because YOU fucked up I actually have to fuck a fucking cripple, AND as I don't have the fucking recipe, the London guys are going to fucking kill ME. After they fucking kill me, they will come after you and kill fucking YOU! Are you getting any of this Bulldog? Are you? We – are – going – to DIE!"

# 6

## The Police… again.

I left club land behind as I tried to angrily march to the town centre as best as I could given my burst blisters and various other trauma pains and broken bits. Debating with myself on how Bulldog stopping for petrol had probably got us both killed.

It was then that I looked up and recognised the rat faced man, leaning against a car. Waiting for me.

"Detective Lovecum," I said. "Fancy seeing you here."

"Cuvlum," he said. He held out a limp paw. "Would you like to fist me?"

"No, I'm really not in the mood for a fisting," I replied.

"Okay, get in the car then." He took the bag from me and passed it through the window to D.I. Short who sat in the front seat. Opening the back door, he gestured for me to get in. I pointed to the direction I was headed and was about to excuse myself when Cuvlum lunged out and bundled me into the car. I felt like a pin-ball, being smashed here and there by people as if they were flashing paddles. I'm at the mercy of others way too much these days and its not fun at all.

I position myself carefully in the car, sitting with my hands on my knees, my carpet burned testicles rubbing against each other again. I can feel the wounds are getting to the sticky stage and my balls have adhered to each other. Getting out of the car is going to hurt like a bastard I thought. Cuvlum climbed in beside me and twisted, as if side-saddle and looked at me. It was awkward, he looked at me for way too long. It looked like he was going to try and kiss me. But at least he wasn't sucking his thumb. "Anything you'd like to say to me?" he said, with a smug grin.

"Your hair looks really nice," I said.

"I told you we'd be watching you," he said. "Big score?"

"Big what?" I said, confused.

"The bag," he said. "What is in the bag? Big score?" D.I. Short handed over the bag, Cuvlum placed it on his lap. "What is in the bag?" he asked again.

"Nothing," I said.

"Nothing?" questioned Cuvlum.

"Clothes."

"So, are you a mule or a money train? Shall we have a look-see?"

I'm dreading him looking in the bag. Black clothes and a balaclava, he will instantly recognise my face when he sees the rape kit. Game over. He will put two and two together and conclude rapist.

"Do you have a search warrant?" I asked.

"Do I need one? Am I in your home?" he said. He then unzipped the bag and thrust his hand in. You'd have thought he'd shoved his hand in shit such was the look on his face. Disappointment did battle with anger as he went through his full range of facial expressions. It was impressive, like an actor doing a show reel. After inspecting the lining, he upturned the bag and spilled the clothes onto his lap. "What's this?" he said angrily.

"I told you, clothes."

He inspected the top in black, then the cargo jeans in black. My heart sank as he found the woollen item of apparel. Inspected it, then worked out what it was. "What do we have here?"

"A balaclava," I said. "Not to be confused with a baklava which is a kind of dessert."

"Don't try to be funny mate. What's the balaclava for? Eh? What's it for?" Cuvlum pressed.

"Beating off."

"Beating off?"

"Yeah, I wanted to look like a Ninja or special forces guy tonight. There is no man alive who wouldn't love to watch a Ninja beat off or meet a special forces guy and beat off with him. We are doing it a bit like WWE wrestling with themes and stuff."

"Themes?"

"Yeah, themes. Doing the fantasies you had as a kid. There is not a kid alive who hasn't dreamed of watching a Ninja fist a special forces marine, then see them beat off."

"Might I inspect the items?" A voice came from the dashboard of the car. Was I stoned? Totally spannered?

Because I'm sure the car just spoke. With that, a guy got out of a van I hadn't noticed parked in front of the car and collected the bag and clothes from Cuvlum. Who the fuck was this guy? I don't need any extra cast members in my life right now for fuck sake.We sat in the car, deep in a very uncomfortable silence. I decided to break it. "So, Cuvlum, if you could fist anyone, who would it be?"

Cuvlum thought deeply for a moment, then ventured, "Mandela, I'd love to fist Nelson Mandela." It was childish I know. I don't know what was more painful, trying not to laugh out loud, my broken insides, my bruised outside or the cast of people I neither knew nor liked dictating my every move. It's like when you have an ulcer in your mouth. Everything you do causes some kind of discomfort, eating, talking, yawning. And you can't help testing it with your tongue, prodding it prompting further agony.

Eventually the bag was returned. I was released and I gingerly got out of the car after enduring another 'We'll be watching you' speech. Back into the drizzle. Both vehicles did a dramatic and rather unnecessary fast pull away, tearing off down the road. I looked up at the grey sky, as the rain fell on my face again. I was wet, exhausted and hungry as fuck. Maybe, I thought, this was how tramps happen. You blunder into a bizarre and fucked up situation like this and everywhere you go people are there to kick you in the nuts. So you just give up, right where you stand, and crawl under a bench to sleep and never come out. Because lets face it, that would probably be a safer option for me right now.

Once again, I'm walking away from a situation not of my choosing. Another vehicle pulls along side.

"Get in."

I was about to yell, 'You know what – fuck off,' but it was Bulldog in the rattiest looking gold Toyota Estima, pursued by a massive and far from discrete white cloud of smoke.

"You followed me in this?"

"Yeah. Wass your point dude?"

"There is a fuckin massive cloud of white smoke belching from it Dog!"

"Yeah, turbo seals going and it's throwing oil down the exhaust manifold."

"So, you didn't think they might notice being followed by a massive white cloud then? Like you are in a fuckin clowns car?"

"Do you have your own car?" Bulldog barked back in defence.

"Point taken," I said. I climbed in and like a long term married couple, we didn't say one word to each other on our journey. We just looked out of the windows, muttering inaudibly under our breaths while exchanging the occasional disapproving look. In total silence except for the thrumb squeak squeek of the windscreen wipers, we returned to the Red Lion pub.

We sat at the same table as before. It seemed the best place to go over how everything had gone tits up. "Hey, its the rapist," said the barman with a smile as I ordered my Guinness. Deep in my thoughts it was pretty bloody

96

clear that things had taken a definite turn for the worse. I had no recipe for the thugs and I'd actually have to fuck Stadnyk's wife. I couldn't fuck her before, there is no way I could get an erection. Then I remembered I couldn't have a wank the night before either. What if my cock actually was really broken and not just traumatized by the thought of beng forced into that orang-utan minge? My head fell into my hands which sent a sharp pain along my bruised back. I was trying to fight back crying my heart out. Things were bad. Very, very bad indeed. "We have to get that recipe," I said.

"I know." Bulldog agreed.

"I know where it is so we'll have to break in and steal it. I can't believe I'm actually saying this, but we'll have to break in to the Ukrainian Maffia's office and steal their recipe for cocaine."

"You can't steal it. He'll know it's gone, you'll have to take a copy of whats on that flash drive dude." Bulldog was right.

"Okay, you pick me up when I'm done raping and I will get in and get a copy."

"Raping?"

"It's not how it sounds, I'm not a real rapist."

"What the fuck does that mean? You yell 'surprise' after you rape someone?" Bulldog looked alarmed.

"Oh, it's not like that. Stadnyk wants me to rape his wife. No, wait, that sounds even worse. His cripple of a wife wants to be raped."

"Dude, that sounds kinda hot!" Bulldog offered.

"Well it ain't," I said. "Which reminds me, can you get other drugs and stuff?"

"Such as?"

"Viagra. Right now there is no way I could fuck her unless I fashioned some kind of splint for my cock out of a couple of lollypop sticks and some duck tape!"

"Yeah, I can get some pukka Viagra. I'll bring your K and I'll bring something else to the party too."

"What?"

"Insurance," he said mysteriously.

We agreed to meet in ASDA's supermarket car park at six. I was to get some blank CD's to copy the files. I turned down the offer of a lift there, choosing to walk. The rain on my face felt cleansing and helped me to think. I couldn't seem to form one solid thought though. I was too exhausted. If I had carried a charity bucket with all the walking I have been doing, I'd have raised thousands of pounds by now. I'm in a lot of pain, and dealing with it in a state of sobriety was not by choice. And just as typical, I'm having to put more miles on my blistered feet.In the supermarket I buy the blank discs, along with a box of painkillers and a packet of indigestion tablets.

Then to the café. I order some scrambled eggs with beans. Foods I hoped might help the Naloxone do its stuff. I added a large cappuccino to my tray.

The girl at the till rang up my order then physically recoiled when she looked at me, "Are you OK? Have you been in a car crash or something?"

"I'm fine," I replied and tried to smile, but all I could muster was a kind of grimace.

"Are you sure your ok?"

"Never better," I replied. I'm sure my tongue found a loose tooth.

Just as I turned to make my way to a table, the cashier chimed again. "Excuse me, sorry to bother you, but, erm don't I know you?" she continued. "You look kinda familiar."

"I get that a lot," I said.

As soon as the food arrived. I punched out the remaining Naloxone pills right on top of the scrambled eggs, just like a kid does with toppings on ice cream. Then I topped that with the whole packet of painkillers. I unravelled the packet of indigestion tablets and dropped all of them, one by one into the coffee. I heaped a fork load of the egg and pill cocktail into my mouth and crunched the contents into an acrid chemical paste. It tasted vile so I painted my egg based pill mountain with tomato ketchup. I shovelled another fork load in my mouth, crunched the mixture and swallowed. Each mouth full was greeted at the stomach with a burning pain so intense I started to sweat. Fuck it I thought. If I'm going to die, it's going to be pain free, so I forked shed loads more into my mouth and forced myself to swallow, and then swallowed some more.

It was then I noticed the old lady opposite, her mouth was open. Her face a mixture of fear and sympathy, looking at me with total shock and horror. I was about to say something but my stomach made a god awful and wet sounding gurgle, loud enough for the whole café to hear. I tried to smile, but the sharp, bitter and acid taste of the pills clashing with the over sweet taste of the ketchup, sent me into a facial spasm. My head curled to the left, trembled and I grimaced. Exhibiting my bruised lip and blood stained teeth. The old lady looked disgusted and left. I ate more of my pharmacy eggs and choked down my chalky coffee.

Time only goes slowly at the times you want it to go fast and only goes fast when you want it to stop. This was one of those times. I wanted to slip into long and comfortable daydreams. I longed for my ugly flat. I wanted to walk over my carpet of dirty cloths, crawl into my own bed, with a duvet and sheet that have been on there so long I think I should buy them a birthday cake. But right now, time was evaporating at an alarming rate, and the evening to come was rushing towards me like a freight train. There was no doubt in my mind that it wasn't a light at the end of a tunnel, it was the fucking freight train about to mow me down.

I knew it was 6pm, or about that, when a thick white cloud descended on the car park outside to the tune of angry horns. People couldn't see to park their cars or back out of the supermarket car park or even walk about. Those that managed to get to the entrance of the store came in coughing with tears streaming down their faces and their hands across their mouths like they were about to vomit. My phone buzzed. It was a text from Bulldog telling me that he had arrived. As if the smoke wasn't a clue. Perfect, I thought, this huge cloud was enough to draw so many eyes in my direction as I walked towards its source that they could all report seeing the rapist getting in a gold Toyota. I'd have been more discrete getting into a UFO. "You get the shit?" I asked.

100

"Yeah." Bulldog offered me a plastic bag with three blue diamond pills.

"This the Viagra?"

"Yeah."

"How many do I take?"

"Don't know dude. Never needed it."

"How long does it take to work?"

"No idea," he said. "But you aint getting your ketamine, you can't take it with those."

I didn't tell him I'd been eating fists full of Naloxone, whole packets of painkillers and a cocktail of caffeine and indigestion tablets. I opened the bag, and swallowed all three. I figured I would need as much help as possible to fuck asparagus legs and besides, if I did die tonight I'm planning on doing it Bruce Willis style. I'm gonna die hard.

"Hey," Bulldog whispered, then looked about as if other people were hiding in his car, and said again, "Hey, look, look at this." From under his seat he withdrew an oiled rag. Unwrapped it, to reveal another oiled rag. Unwrapped that, and on his lap was a massive revolver. "What the fuck is that?" I asked.

"It's a Webly Fosbery," he said.

"Fuck me, its enormous. You steal it off Hellboy?"

"Nah. Looks fuckin scary though huh?" Bulldog countered.

"Looks antique," I replied. "Where did you get it?" Bulldog handed me the revolver. It was so heavy I almost needed both hands to lift it. It was solid, cold and felt like compressed death.

"It was my Granddad's, he used it in the Boar War."

"The what?" I asked.

"The Boar war, it was the war between the first world war and the second. Grandad fought in it's last year, 1902."

"Fuck me, it's an antique. You might as well have brought a fuckin musket."

"Fuck you, this is my insurance," Bulldog was annoyed. "A gun is a gun mate. Point this at someone and they do what the fuck you tell em."

"Yeah, suppose your right. Sorry dude. Does it work?"

"No idea."

"Do you have bullets?"

"Only the ones in it. Don't know how to cock it to check. But Granddad kept it loaded, he was afraid after the war."

"Of what, King Kong?" I said as I returned the oversized pistol. "Fuck it," I said, "I have to go back in the store, I need a torch."

"I've got one in here," Bulldog said. He searched about below his seat and passed me a fuck off torch. It looked like a thermos flask with a giant showerhead attached. I thought better than to mock the Dog further for fear of him telling me to fuck off.

And so we planned again. Bulldog drops me off for a quick rape, waits for me, drives me too Stadnyk's office. Bulldog keeps look out. We set our phones to silent, synchronise watches. Break in, copy flash drive, call thugs, call police. Simple enough.

# 7

## Fuck-work with attitude (and a bit of rapage)

We drove to where asparagus legs lived. And waited till 7.30. Bulldog asked if he could do the rape, which was a bit weird. I said no. I explained that I'll have to take off the balaclava afterwards and look at the camera, so that she knows it was me. With that there was a tingling, hydraulic sensation. My cock was getting harder and harder, as if litres of blood was being pumped in. "Fuck me, this Viagra shit works eh?" I said.

"No idea dude, told ya I aint got your problem," Bulldog replied.

"What problem? I don't need them usually. Don't ask me why but I just don't get turned on by being forced to rape fugly fat cripples."

"What ever you say dude. What ever you say," he replied.My cock was getting Chuck Norris hard. I couldn't sit normally in the back of the Toyota any more. I had to kind of slouch along the back seat. I grabbed Stadnyk's bag of clothes and started to get changed. I decided no shoes, just socks. So I can whip em off quick and fuck. Maybe that was the problem last time, it wasn't the horror, simply that I still had my shoes on? I took off my jeans. Then, thinking about quick and instant access, I decided to go commando and removed my boxers too. I have to say my cock was hard as hell, and my God did it look impressive. I had to fight the temptation to show it to Bulldog. I did however, take a picture with my phone. Just in case a girl is ever interested I'll have a record of it at it's best. I then thought of sending it to you Mia, with the note 'look what your missing' but that was probably the only thing you didn't leave me for. My cock was so hard, I wondered if I could just run in with my cock out and harpoon it straight in so I didn't have to look. But then she might have clothes on and I'd look stupid.

I slipped on the Black cargo jeans, the long sleeve top and balaclava. And waited. Bulldog suggested, wisely, that maybe I should wait to put the balaclava on once I got in the house, as it didn't look too clever to be sat outside a complex of rich peoples homes in a balaclava. So I took it off.So, there we sat, Bulldog armed with a giant antique gun and me armed with an engorged penis, waiting for 7.30. My cock started to throb and was hard as a diamond. With all the recent blood loss, I was a little concerned that I wouldn't have enough for my hard-on and the rest of my body.7.30 came and its time for me to give the performance of my life. Still, I thought, I've got a fucking grate prop. Again I admire my temporary tan in the gold mirrored lift on my trip up to the penthouse. When all this is over, and I'm not dead. I might invest in a spray tan. The lift stops, opens and I exit. In front is 8c. My cock feels huge and fat, like a sex marrow. So no floppy cock worries there then. But, the thought of asparagus legs and her road kill vagina is still off putting. I am a victim of circumstance and this fuck is for freedom.I put on the balaclava and approach the door which is slightly a jar. I start to push it open and its all dark and silent inside except for the hum of some appliance within, must be a fridge or something. Then I think, what sort of rapist am I? Do I say anything? Do I talk dirty? Am I an angry rapist? Should I maybe make animal noises? I realise that I'm not totally sure what rapists do. I'm a wanted rapist who hasn't raped but who is about to rape but doesn't want to. I sneak in, close the door behind me and its dark. I creep into the bedroom, and there she is. She looks even bigger than before. She looks like Shamoo in a tracksuit, lying prone on the bed. Fuck me, she didn't even try to dress up for me. I'm a little pissed off but I suppose she was being considerate coz a tracksuit should be easy to remove. I wish I had some ketamine to kill of all of my senses, mute the limbic cortex of my brain and auto pilot through this shit.

I stood there, pleased that the ghastly scene was lit only through a chink in the curtains. I look over to where the phone was, but the table had been cleared, and something with a red light on is in it's place. I lean over and inspect it and it's the video camera. This was a sharp reminder that this was fucking real and I'd better fucking get on with the fucking. Trying not to think about what I was doing I lunged for her waist band, and yanked. Her tracksuit bottoms slipped down but only by about an inch. So I yanked again, then again, but even harder. She was so heavy they hadn't moved hardly at all. So I grabbed her tracksuit at her ankles and tugged. Nothing. Fuck me, had she super glued em on? So I tugged away like I was in a tug of war, gripping with all my might and violently pulling and yanking. Each time, she slid down the bed, along with the bed cover. After a good five minutes of ripping at her bottoms, I was starting to sweat and the woollen balaclava was making my whole head itch. I let go of her tracksuit, and her crippled legs thudded to the floor.I didn't want to get close or do anything intimate, but I had to inspect the reason for my undress failings. I lifted her top, revealing her large belly gathered like a Christmas cracker at the waistband. Everything was kind of puckered together and stretched. With one hand I lifted her folds of fat and could see the reason the tracksuit was still in place. A drawstring. My yanking had tightened it like a noose. Fuck, I thought, I hope she is paralysed at the hips, because this would hurt like fuck in the morning. I pulled at the bow, and she doubled in width as she unfurled. The bottoms were huge, like a marquee. I grabbed the material and yanked, and this time they came free. I tried to pull them off, but forgot she had shoes on. So now I had the shoe inside the trouser issue. I mean its bad enough when its your own shoe stuck in your jeans because your so drunk that you've tried to get your kecks off without removing your shoes first. If you have shoes you can slip off then your okay, but if their lace ups, your kinda fucked and you need to pull your jeans up remove the shoes and then off with the jeans. My problem now was that I hadn't a fucking clue what kind of shoes she had on.So I massaged the foot inside the fabric, like I was trying to guess a Christmas present. It felt like a trainer, but I couldn't feel laces. By the size of her, it might have been a hoof I was feeling and she goes to a blacksmith when she needs shoes. I pulled at the heel and tried to lift the shoe free. It gave a little, so I tried harder. No way was I going to try pull her trousers up to take off the shoe, her calves should have been in a field. So I struggled with all my might. There was a little snapping noise like stiches being ripped and then I noticed that the toe of the shoe was touching the front of her leg. Fuck I think I've probably snapped her ankle. But she's paralysed, so fuck it, I carried on wrestling with the foot. Even if I did snap her ankle, can you break what's already broke?

Finally, the shoe came free, revealing a big, puffy foot. I think I would have preferred to find a hoof. Her foot was so ugly and smelt so bad that I involuntarily recoiled, showing my gums. She looked like dough, all lumpy and white in the darkness. I let go of her leg, and the foot flopped loose like a faulty supermarket trolley wheel.Her huge panties were around her knees. They looked like a dirty parachute. I yanked them off. I'm sure they were wet, and there was an overbearing mushroom smell. I didn't want to stop, I didn't want to think, I just wanted it over. I'm a cripple raper. A fat, cripple raper. I lifted her legs. They felt like two long heavy balloons full of mince meat, all lumpy, floppy and falling at odd angles. I slid her closer to the edge of the bed.

I yanked down my trousers, and I was still hard as hell. I kind of hoped the camera caught it, because it was so damned impressive. Such a shame it was going to be wasted here. I edged closer. My cock was magnificent, her vagina looked like a grenade had exploded in a skip full meat, and her skin felt fake, cold and pimply like a plucked raw turkey. I moved closer and tried to place myself in her. But I got snagged in one of her many dry fleshy curtains. I tried again. I tried to force it in with all the strength I could muster but that just buckled my shaft and hurt my helmet. Her fanny was massive, you could shove both your hands in it and still have enough room to shuffle a deck of cards. But it was as dry as a bucket of sand. I tried to spit on it, but I was so disgusted with myself, I couldn't get any get any saliva. I looked about the room for some kind of lubricant. I checked the bedside table. Nothing. I checked the dressers drawers and shelves, still nothing. This was taking way too long, and I wanted to be out of there.

I ran into the bathroom and looked through her cabinets, nothing. I found a bottle of hair conditioner and considered it, that was superseded by shampoo. Bubbles I thought. She might not like to see a massive twat-froth on the video.

108

A *'cuntachino'* I called it. I know, its not a word. I tried the kitchen. Getting desperate, I looked in the fridge and found the answer. I returned to the bedroom with a tub of margarine. I popped the lid, scooped a big handful out, and plastered her vagina with it. It felt like I was trying to ice a gibbon's mouth. But it worked. And I slammed my cock in.On my scale of low points. I think I'd reached the bottom. Trying to dry hump a cripple, and lubing it with something pretending to be butter. I'm trying not to think, as I'm hammering away. I'm fucking as fast as I can, pistoning in and out. I'm not sure if it's all the painkillers, the viagra, the Naloxone, or a the combination of all three, but I cant feel a thing. I'm trying to get this over with, fucking as fast as I can to blow my load in her, as requested, but my cock is numb, I cant feel anything. Nothing. Nadda. I could be here all night. It feels like the balaclava is eating my face from the heat and sweat from my vigorous fucking. On and on, with no sensation that I was going to cum. Faster, I thought. So I smashed away at her even quicker. It sounded like I was punching a bucket of raw liver.Exhausted I stopped, hands on my hips, like I'd been running a marathon, with my cock still in her, panting like a dog in the sun. When my heart rate retuned to a reasonable level but still having to breathe through my mouth, I was off again. Stadnyk couldn't knock my work ethic, I was shagging like my life depended on it. Because it did. What felt like an hour in, the friction, sweat and margarine gave off the sent of baking. But it still felt like I was fucking her with a stolen dick. Stuff this I thought, there must be enough margarine in there to bung her up for a month. I'm done. I grunted like a troll as I faked an orgasm. There was no way she'd know.I pulled out, my cock all veiny and oiled with margarine. Her big, buttered gash gaping open like a big hairy handbag. I kind of wished she'd wake up so I could at least show my cock to someone, it looked fucking marvellous. I had to kind of fold it into my jeans before I zipped up. I was still diamond hard. I pulled off my balaclava, leaned into the video camera for a close up and did a cocky salute and winked. I grabbed my top and then ran the fuck out of there.I found it bloody hard to run with my erection. I'm not sure anyone has ever had to run with an erection before, but if they had, they'd tell you it's not easy. You have to kind of run all hunched over.

I slid back the door on Bulldog's people carrier and jumped in the back. Bulldog was leaning over the seat, like an expectant father, "Well?"

"Well what?"

"How was it?" he asked.

"What?" I couldn't believe he was actually asking.

"It. Her. Was it good?"

"She was a heavily sedated cripple, how the fuck do you think it was?"

"Yeah, but raping, tell me about the rape bit, what was that like?"

"She was heavily sedated, so didn't move a muscle, show any emotion or display any pleasure. It was exactly like normal sex" I said.

# 8

## Breaking and entering.

I figured Stadnyk's office, above the lock-up, sat behind nightclubs would be quiet. As the night drew on, the thumping music and revellers would be distraction enough. For all the carnage and activity at the front of clubs, the rear is usually isolated and deserted. At least that was my experience when the transvestite tried to smash my face off with her cock. I'd never done any burglary before. B & E as they call it. I would have been terrified had I not felt so dog shit tired. We decided on 12am. 1am folks start to leave the clubs, 11pm is too early as they would be going into the clubs as the pubs started to shut. We deemed midnight to be the ideal burglary threshold. Bulldog parked the Toyota up the street. It was very well lit, and that put me off but Bulldog remembered something from his school days and ran over to the first streetlight. He sort of hugged the base and started rocking it, the rhythm of the rocking made the lamp swing wildly and then as if by magic, the light went out. He did the same to the remaining two lights and the area plunged into darkness. We sat waiting, watching and casing the joint. Leaving the engine running for a quick getaway was one idea but the resulting cloud of white smoke would mean we wouldn't see the cast of Starlight Express if they turned up on their flashing rollerskates.

My heart was trying to punch its way out of my chest. Adrenalin works better than any speed. I would collapse from fatigue were it not for my own body's endocrine system straight lining me a range of chemicals. As 12 approached we said less, favouring to re-run the scenario in our heads, reassuring ourselves that the plan was safe and sound. The truth was that the plan was at best flimsy and at worst suicidal. The only thing to speak was my stomach which made long intermittent noises like water gurgling down a plug hole.

Soon my penis and my watch hands had synchronised as 12 arrived. All standing to attention. "Okay," I said. "This is it, keep your eyes open I'm going in."

"No worries," said Bulldog, waving his pistol. "I've got your back."

I have to admit that the sight Bulldog's massive gun did make me feel a bit better. Balaclava on, I slid the door of the Toyota open. Outside I could hear the distant thuds of the clubs base drums, far off laughter and boy racer cars roaring up roads. The temperature had dropped. I tried to get a better view of the building, but it was completely bathed in darkness. I ran over, ducking in doorways. As I approached the building I remembered the entrance I came in and out of at Stadnyk's office. It was an emergency door with one of those bars you push to open it. On the outside I couldn't see a key hole, handle, nothing. Just a big solid door. Next to the door was a large roller shutter. How the fuck do I get in? As my eyes better adjusted to the dark I noticed that there was a door within the roller shutter. It was fastened shut with a bolt which was locked with a fuck off big padlock. The first floor had windows and it looked like one was open, but I couldn't get up there. Epic fail, I can't get in. I abort the mission and run back to the car.

"Got it?" Bulldog asked.

"Course I haven't you twat, it's like fort fuckin knox."

"Well what did you expect, for them to leave a door open for you or a key under a fucking welcome mat?"

"No, but I didn't expect burglary to be this hard. You see the guys in the paper who get arrested and they look like right thick cunts," I said.

"Well, they are, that's why they got caught." Bulldog shot me an 'obviously' stare. "Let me look." With that, he jumped out of the Toyota and had accompanied me most of the way to the building when I remembered I'd forgotten the torch, so we ran back to the car again. All this running was playing havoc with my cock. Still hard as hell, I should have tried to pry the door open with it. All the running was making the zipper on the jeans rub my tip raw.

"Got it?" asked Bulldog.

"I have now," I confirmed.

"Ready?" He asked.

"Yeah, lets do this." Bulldog ran off to the building, I did a hunched over semi-run. I was Quasimodo, trying to protect my dick from being chewed off by the jeans and stop my carpet burned testicles from clattering together. Bulldog is scoping the place and I'm looking about but fuck knows what for.

"Hey," I loud whisper. "You got a hair pin or wire or something like that?"

"What the fuck would I be doing with a hair pin? Why?" Bulldog asked.

"Thought I'd try to pick the lock."

"Can you pick locks?" he asked.

"Don't know. Never tried." Bulldog just looked at me. "Yeah, suppose if it was that easy, padlocks would be pretty redundant." The adrenalin was dropping as my frustration rose.

Then, Bulldog got excited. "I've an idea, wait here." And with that, he ran off into the distance, and enveloped into the blackness. It was so quiet I could hear my own breathing. Then Bulldog returned, running toward me.

"Stand back," he ordered. I then noticed it in his hand, bigger than my monster torch, he was holding the revolver.

"You going to hold the building ransom?" I asked sarcastically.

"Nope," he replied, waving the pistol like a mexican bandit. "Gonna shoot the lock off like in the movies."Bulldog stood in front of the lock, arms out stretched and pointed the gun

114

at the steel clasp. I waited with excitement. Nothing happened. "Go on then," I said.

"I'm trying. It wont work."

"Is the safety on?"

"Fucked if I know. Hang on," Bulldog fiddled with the gun and pointed it right at me. I dived out of the way. "Think that's it." He assumed the position again, barrel of the gun a mere inch from the lock. I pressed against the wall, eyes shut, waiting for the bang. Nothing. I opened my eyes and he was still standing there. I stood beside him, looking at the lock and at the pistol. We stood there a while, I watched him fiddling with the revolver, pulling at some bits and pushing others. There was a click as he pulled back the hammer and primed the gun. "Ah-ha," he said. 'Got the bastard.' I must admit, I had little faith, what works after a hundred years? He pointed the barrel so close it almost touched the padlock. Point blank, Dog pulled the trigger.There was an almighty BANG. We were both temporarily bleached white by the guns massive explosion. The power sent Bulldog tumbling to the ground. And in that same instant, sent the bullet, the scolding hot bullet, through my shoulder.

"Ahhhhhghh, fuck I'm hit!" I collapsed on the floor.

"What?" shouted Bulldog. I could hardly hear him my ears were ringing. The air was thick with the pungent smell of burnt cordidite.

"You shot me you cunt, you fucking shot me in the arm."I ran off, holding my arm, bent over because my cock was hurting as much as the gunshot wound. Maybe, all the blood in my cock would stop me bleeding to death. I could make out the sound of footsteps in pursuit and hoped it was Bulldog but frankly, I didn't give a damn. I'd been shot. I slumped against the van and then slid to the ground. I took my hand off the wound and it was wet with blood. I felt dizzy.

"Dude," Bulldog says as he slid back the door on the Toyota, slamming it into the back of my head.

"Oww, stop trying to fuckin murder me you cunt."

"Sorry." Bulldog was flapping in a panic. "I can't have shot you dude, I was aiming at the lock." I climbed in. I reclined across the back seats and pulled my arm out of my rapist top to inspect my shoulder. There was a deep puncture wound, about the size of a pencil tip and thick dark blood oozing out. It looked like a jam doughnut.

"Must be a fragment of the padlock in there," Bulldog continued. "The gun must have blown it to bits."

"Fuck this!" I moaned. "I want to go home. Enough. I'm done. I'd rather do time for rape or take my chances proving it wasn't me. It has to be better than being shot and beaten up all the time."

"Look, the locks off now mate, we're home and free. Just run in and copy the files and we are both in the clear." Bulldog presented some truth. If not for me, for him. I had to go in.

After a short rest we ran back to the building. Jeans still eating my cock. I inspected the lock, and it was perfectly intact. Not a scratch. If anything it looked shinier. "What the fuck?" I shouted. My heart sank. Bulldog looked at it and shrugged. The ancient bullet must have shattered on impact, sending shrapnel into my arm. We were no closer to getting in. Bulldog ran to the side of the building and looked up at the window. "Too high," I said. But Bulldog started to fashion a sort of ladder from discarded wooden pallets. I decided the best option was to try and force open the firedoor. I could get my fingers on the bottom edge. I yanked at it, and it gave a little, providing me with more of an edge. I could just about slide my fingers under, but it was a very tight fit. By the fingernails, I pulled. I pulled with all my might, knowing that the leverage, if I could free more of the door and use it, would pop the lock. My effort gave me about a quarter inch more. I pushed more of my fingers under and pulled as fiercely as I could. Slowly the door was opening.

There was a muffled voice. I couldn't make out what it said. "Bulldog?" I shouted.

"STAND BACK?" it replied. Was he inside?

The door flew open. Or it would have done had it not trapped my fingers under it before smashing my face. Bulldog had got in through the window and kicked the bar to open the door not knowing my fingers were underneath and were now crushed. As the door had not opened wide, he booted it again.

"AAAAAGHHHH, pull the door," I cried. "PULL THE FUCKING DOOR!" My fingers were flattened below the hard wood. I tried to pull them free but they were jammed. It was agony. Bulldog tried to look through the gap, like Johny from the shining. "What?" He asked.

"Pull the fucking door, my fingers are trapped under the door."

"What?" he said again.

"The door. Pull the fucking door. My fingers are trapped. PULL THE FUCKING DOOR!" I was becoming hysterical.

Bulldog pulled the door, but it was stuck, held in place by my fingers. Bulldog kept tugging at it and with each effort the door retreated a little more, taking my fingers with it. Each time he tugged at the door I had to try and yank my fingers free, shaving off more of the skin with each tug. Slowly the door dragged away, and as it did it further ruined my fingers. Once again we retreated to the Toyota, but this time leaving an open door behind us. And this time I ran while crying. It was all too much. The beatings, the blisters, the ruined guts, the gunshot, my penis getting wittled and now my fucked up fingers.

There was a sense of Déjà vu, we were back in the Toyota, I was on the back seat and bleeding. I inspected my hand under the dull yellow of the interior light of the car. One nail split, and ribbons of grazes, decorated with little pieces of gravel and dirt. "How is it?" Bulldog asked.

"How do you think? You crushed my fuckin fingers."

"Sorry dude," Bulldog offered. "But at least we can get in now and close the door behind us without the Ukrainian guys knowing we are there."

"How did you make it up to the window?"

"Found a ladder."

"A ladder? Where?"

"Yeah. Lucky huh? Was just lying there in the corner along the wall the window was in."

This gave me a pang of alarm. "Don't you think that's just a bit convenient?"

"Nah. What kind of idiot would want to break in the Ukrainian Mafia's office? It's just luck dude." He didn't see the irony in what he had just said. The adrenalin was keeping me going and now I had access. We sat in silence for a while, collecting our thoughts, readying our nerves. With no obstacles in place, I had nothing to stop me. I was moments from freedom. All I had to do was get in, copy the files and go. Simple.

I casually walk toward the building. Pause by the entrance. Then, after a quick check, I sprinted in, closing the door behind me. I was a little amazed there was no alarm. Immediately on my left was an entrance to the area inside the roller doors. In front, the long concrete stairway I had climbed before. I made my way up the stairs, the windows facing the street were slightly illuminated by the remaining streetlights. As my eyes adjusted to the darkness, progress was easy. Atop the stairs, things were different than I remember. Bigger. It's amazing how little you digest when you are not truly paying attention. There were three rooms that looked like offices, and one room that looked like a storage, kitchen area. Its amazing how your other senses compensate for the lack of vision, sound taking up the deficit of lack of vision. The silence was deafening. Also I could smell cleaning products, the place smelled old yet sterile.

I opened the door to the first office. I could hear the gentle whirring of some electrical device, like a computer tuned on. The desk was small and different. I could hear my heart beating, and could hear my breathing. I was amped up on fear. I exited the small office and went to the large door in the centre. I tested the cold metal handle, and silently, the spring loaded handle fell and the door opened. This was the room. The familiar smell of cigar and aftershave clung to the air, even in total darkness I would have known this was Stadnyk's office. There was his desk. There was the sofa I was on before. The room was much bigger than I remembered. This was the right room though. I could feel my blood pumping through my veins. I also felt a disturbing sensation that something had moved in my bowls. Like a giant heavy knot of compacted intestine had been cut free and fallen into my colon. I had a warm tickly wave like sensation rush though my body. There was definitely movement in my guts, they were doing somersaults. I approached Stadnyk's desk. I tried the drawers, and amazingly, they slid open. First drawer, glasses case, post it notes, a locked box. I hoped too fuck the drive wasn't in there. Second drawer, packet of cigars, a journal and would you believe it, a silver flash drive. The silver fucking flash drive.

At last a break. I had an uplifting sensation that things would be okay, quickly followed by a warm and wet feeling that the sensation in my gut was going to become an issue. What ever the blockage was, it had moved itself into the departures lounge area of my ass. I looked for the hard drive to power it on, but couldn't find it. I looked under the desk, in the large drawer but there wasn't one. But there had to be. The hard drive hadn't been removed because the monitor was still on the desk, as was the keyboard, so there would have been cables attached to nothing, hanging down. So where was it? I even checked the carpet for the impression left from where a computer once stood. Nothing.

I inspected the monitor, recognised the fruit logo, an apple. It was an imac. Hard drive and monitor in one. Result. I withdrew the CD from my pocket, took the flash drive and... how the fuck do you turn it on? I suddenly felt like, at last, I needed to take a shit. I was relieved from the knowledge that it's starting to work in there again, but cursed the timing. I also cursed not wearing underwear. My cock was so sore.

I inspected the keyboard, but couldn't see any way to turn the computer on. I inspected the computer itself but the back of it being black, in this very dark room, I couldn't make out the bumps and textures for buttons. So I reached for Bulldogs torch. I found the switch and clicked it on, and it was as if the sun landed in the office. Ridiculously bright light painted everything white, with the exception of the jet black shade, cast from the objects the light hit. I could see cubes of light stencilled on the walls outside, opposite the office, such was the power of the light. The office looked like it was ready for an aircraft to land in it. The torch was so powerful, that the instant brightness burned my eyes like I was staring at the sun. I shut my eyes to kill the discomfort but the power of the light was so fierce it punched through my eyelids so I could see purple. I eventually managed to turn the torch off and when I opened my eyes all I could see was green. I would have been more discrete if I'd tried to burgle the office as a one man band.

As soon as the green-ness dissipated and normal vision returned, I placed my hand over the lens of the light to subdue it, and inspected the mac. On the back, in the bottom left corner was an on button. I pressed it and the mac chimed as it whirred into life.

My thigh buzzed. I checked the phone and it was Bulldog. "Yeah," I whispered.

"I can see the light, maybe best not use it."

"You could have told me it was the Olympic bleedin torch. Just keep your eyes peeled OK?"

I found a USB slot, slid in the silver drive, it's contents popped up on the screen 'Recipe' it was called. I found the CD slot, slid in the disk. It too popped up on screen named 'untitled'. This was easy. I'd be in and out in a flash. This was particularly good, as I really, urgently needed a shit. I opened the recipe folder, dragged all the contents across to the disk and hit 'burn'. A window appeared and informed me of the time remaining for the process.

My thigh buzzed again. "What?" I whispered.

"Turn the light off, I can still see it."

"What are you on about, it's not on."

There was a deathly quiet pause before Bulldog continued. "Are you downstairs?"

"No," I said

"Oh fuck dude, they are in there. Get out. Get out like NOW!"

"I can't," I said. "It's not copied yet, I'm in the office."

"Hide!"

I looked about the office, it was void of any place to hide except under the desk and that was the very place you would go to in an almost empty office. "Okay, stay on the phone dude." I needed contact. I was scared witless. I flipped the mac so it was face down on the desk to hide the glow. And got under the desk.

And then I heard it. Shouting. I couldn't make out the words but I didn't have to. Someone was pleading and two other voices were aggressively asserting themselves. Screaming came from downstairs, followed by blood curdling thuds. The begging and pleading continued and the slapping noises were relentless. Laughing and jeers vied for space in my ears with screams. Some ones delight at another's clearly severe pain turned my blood cold. I couldn't see what was happening, and thanked god for that. My heart stopped. I was about to check the computer to see if the CD had burnt when I heard footsteps ecko around the stairwell. They were coming upstairs. What if they came in here? No question I would be discovered and the gravity and the seriousness of the situation I had put myself in hit me like a hammer to the head. I started hyperventilating, I was trapped. I pulled up the hem of my top and stretched it over my balaclavered mouth to muffle the sound of my breathing, I was panting with fear and I couldn't stop. The footsteps grew closer, I could hear two men chirping to each other in what I assumed was Ukrainian. They walked passed the office to the further end of the hall, toward the kitchen area. Then I heard more footsteps accompanied by moans and the sound of something being dragged. I peered over the desk as they went past the open door of Stadnyk's office. The vision before me turned my blood to ice. Stadnyk walked in front, in a white doctor style coat, spattered with blood. Holding onto a guy by what appeared to be a strap-on cock fastened to his head. Stadnyk's legs were bare. The beaten and tortured mans hands were cuffed behind his back and he had what looked like a horses bit between his teeth, buckled in place by straps. Clearly he'd been beaten. Stadnyk's Mr Enormous was just behind his boss. Huge in the sort of leather biker guy, gay dungeon master look, he was in a sleeveless leather jacket making his bulging muscles look almost cartoon like. However, the display of power was frightning, he was pretty much carrying the handcuffed man being lead by the dildo. The guy resisted walking but his feet were just dragging on the floor.

They walked on past to the nextdoor office. I knew Stadnyk would be in here at some point. If I could slip out of this office, too the hall and out the window Bulldog got in through I would be okay. But this was my only chance to get the recipe and while my odds were low that never bothered me when I was in the seedy casinos in town. I chose to wait for the disk to finish being copied and take it from there. More muffled moans, then, "Okay, OKAY I'll do it." I dread to think what was going on.

But the fear, or maybe the Naloxone or whatever kicked in big time. I couldn't wait. I was about to shit myself.

"Bulldog," I whispered. "I need to shit."

"What? Now?"

"Yeah now," I replied. "I'm gonna shit myself!"

"Can't you wait?"

Truth was, I couldn't. I was no longer the captain of my asshole. A massive stool was breaking for freedom. If I shit in his office, it wouldn't be hard for Stadnyk to know someone had been in there. Fuck, it felt massive, like a head was pushing out of my arse. Then I had another panic. My Viagra cock. Even if I found a discrete place to shit, I'd piss like a fireman's hose, all over the walls. Desperately I searched for answers.

"I'm shitting now," I said.

"Gross," he replied.

"Mate, I don't want them recognising the car, fuck off up the street and I'll meet you there in a while."

"Why?"

"If I'm chased or I'm seen, you don't want to be part of it."

"Okay. I'll wait for you at McDonalds at the top of town."

"Okay," I said, and shut off my phone.

I could hear a computer fire up, followed by tapping of keys. "Everything." I recognised Stadnyk's voice. A conversation took place in Ukrainian, but with long silent pauses, so I assumed Stadnyk was on the phone. After a period of keystrokes, there was a heavy slap, as skin viciously connected with skin. And then the screams were again muffled. I was literally shitting myself with fear. I could hear more violence and what and what I now believe murder sounds like. I had to shit while they were distracted, but its not like I had a choice, my bowels were evacuating without my consent. I searched about the office as quietly as I could for a place to shit, such as a plant pot maybe. Nothing. Then I saw the big expensive apple juice bottle. I gulped down the juice, grabbed handfulls of paper from the printer and returned to Stadnyk's desk. I opened the bottom drawer and lined it with the paper, dropped my trousers and crouched over it. I didn't have to try to expel the turd, it was rolling out of me like the boulder from Indiana Jones. I didn't even think about taking my shoes off. There was a heavy thud, as a solid, compacted stool clumped down like a paperweight. I put the eye of my penis against the large aperture of the bottle and filled it with hot foamy piss, almost to the top. I can't begin to describe the relief.

I looked into the drawer and there it sat, like a bowling ball. I put the bottle on the side and I felt about a stone lighter.

I could hear a rhythm of slaps, too quick in succession for punches. I had to look through the blinds of the window between the offices to see if they were adequately distracted. There was a horror show taking place, bare ass cheeks, thrusting in and out. I hate to think what depravity was going on but maybe they were sadomasochistic and this is what they did for fun. I didn't want to find out, I wanted to get out. Right then, the mac spewed out the disk. It had finished copying the file.

I pressed the off switch till the computer died and, to the sound of men dry-humping, gently returned the mac to it's upright position. I placed the disk in my pocket and returned the flashdrive to it's home in the drawer. My eyes wandered to the shit in the drawer below, I couldn't just leave it there. I looked for something to put it in, a bag or maybe a cup. The only thing I could find was cling-film. Far from ideal, but it was all that there was. I rolled out a length of the plastic sheet, tore it off, and grabbed my shit. It could have been a large baked potato, such was it's size weight and warmth. I picked it up and wrapped it like it was lunch. I got more cling-film and wrapped it again then placed it in the pocket of the cargo jeans. All I had left to do was get out unnoticed.

While they were doing what ever it was they were doing, I went to the open door, Ninja style. I considered the window but also considered the possibility of getting trapped. Besides, there were solid concrete stairs to allow a silent exit, as long as I could get to them. My heart was racing.

If they came out of their room they would have a clear view of the stairs. I just hoped they were busy being perverted. Slowly I crept into the hall. Then to the stairs. I stopped at the top and listened. Still the slapping noises. Slowly I descended towards the firedoor. I peeked outside. All was quiet, I couldn't see anyne. Rather than run and draw the attention of any of Stadnyk's men who might be outside, I casually walked out of the building.

And a way through the dark. I was euphoric but remained calm on the outside so that I wouldn't draw attention to myself. I'd done it. I had actually burgled the Ukrainian Mafia. I took a paved route between two clubs and out into the orange night amongst the revellers and clubbers littering the pavement as some queued to get in and others chased taxi's. I was high on relief. Once I felt far enough away I called Bulldog. "Dude. I've got it!"

"Oh my God." He sounded relieved, "That is fuckin sweet man, you out?"

"Yeah, and I no longer have a shit problem," I laughed. Bulldog laughed too. "Where is the shit now?"

"I have it. It's wrapped. I have a big wrap of shit." I was laughing even harder and it felt great. It seemed like I hadn't laughed for ages.

"You have wrapped shit?" Bulldog scoffed.

"Yep, its huge, and I am gonna give it to you as a thank you present."

"Well at least you can't moan about not having shit for ages," he said.

"I know, mate, you don't know how much you need it, it's agony waiting days for it."

Then I noticed it. I wasn't alone. Amongst the randomness of drunken folk, walking in groups, falling out of taxi's, arguing or queuing, someone else was walking alone, maintaining the same hurried pace as me, they kinda stood out. I turned and took a route that wasn't a thoroughfare. Just to check. There would be no reason to go the way I was going, except to follow me. And the man, a discrete few paces behind me, did just that. "Fuck, Bulldog. I'm being followed."

"WHAT?" he said. "Your kidding."

"There is someone following me, oh shit, oh shit. Go home dude. Go home now!" I said. "If I make it to my house then I'll call you." The man behind me started to sprint, I heard his footsteps getting closer. So I ran too, but my cock was getting ripped apart by my jeans, it was agony. I had no choice. While running, I unzipped my cock and let it out. And I was off, sprinting up the road with my cock out, wagging in front of me. The cool night air breathing on my abraded tip was soothing, my stomach didn't hurt any more, I was like a greyhound. I could hear I was loosing the guy behind me as I jumped a bench then over a wall. I could hear the man behind struggle with the wall. Running as fast as I could, my Viagra cock still wagging in front, I nearly fell as I hit wet grass. For better traction I leapt to a pavement and ran through a car park before making it back onto the well lit streets that filtered to the clubs. People were cheering, clapping and shouting. "Hey, his cock's out!", "Pass us your batton mate!" as I hammered up the road.

I could hear the pursuer shouting behind me. "Go, go, go, he's making a run for it." I had made a huge error running back to the road. A van screeched up in front of me, quickly followed by a police car. I tried to stop and as I did, the policeman following me hit me from behind, smashing me to the ground. I think he snapped my cock.

The guy knelt on my back and cuffed me. If my cock wasn't broken before, it was now. He stood me upright. I turned. It was Detective Short.

"Can you put my cock away for me please?" I said to him.

Short looked down at my cock, then back at me, "I'm not touching it," he said.

"But I'm cuffed," I said. With that, I was stuffed into the car. Cuvlum was already inside.

"Hello again," he plummed.

I was told that I did not have to say anything, however anything I did say would be admissible and the rest of the Amanda shite. My hands were still cuffed behind my back and my cock was still out looking like it should have a flag flying from it. Detective Short got in the front of the car, yelling, "We've got ya now," as he did so. A uniformed officer drove the police car, tearing along the busy nightlife streets, blue lights flashing. He kept taking corners way to fast and I kept falling on my face, the cuffing making it impossible to stop it. It had to be deliberate. And it really hurt my hard on.

# 9

## The Police, drugs and shit:

Briskly I was walked up a ramp to the rear of the station, like a naughty boy by an angry mum. Detective Cuvlum kept saying, "We have you now sunny boy," and, "Soon we will know where Mr. Big is." Was he calling ME Mr. Big? I know my viagra enhanced oily penis was impressive, but was it really worth calling me Mr. Big?

Different desk sergeant, same desk. There I am on the wall, my wanted poster, with a biro moustache and glasses. I'm made to sit in the communal waiting area. There is a woman with a snarling grin that says, "They caught you eh – RAPIST." Detective Cuvlum and several other plain and uniformed officers kept looking over, then looking at their watches, then looking back at me.

After a while two uniformed policemen collected me and asked me to accompany them even as they man handled and shoved me down the corridor. We walked along, past the interview room, past a mews of offices. There was an angry shoutey voice and banging up ahead, and we were heading for it. Down we went along a white tiled corridor to a suite of cells. Each one had a big dark green door with little observation flaps at eye level. There were two male policemen there, who were pinning down some guy who was freaking out on the floor of his cell. The banging and screaming was coming from another cell adjacent to it. A third uniformed officer, an older looking woman, greeted us with a beaming smile.

"Who do we have here?" I was looking terrified at the door being hammered from inside and the accompanied screaming. "Don't worry luv, he's just a drunk," she said, trying to calm the rabbit in the headlights look I knew I had. "Be asleep within the hour, I guarantee it. It's not his first time with us."

I was searched. As they patted me down for what I assume was weapons or needles, one officer patted my cock. "What's this?" he asked.

"My erection," I replied. He gave me a slightly disturbed sideways stare, then in a very matter of fact fashion, continued with his patting. Everything on me was removed, phone, keys, change, the lot and placed into a yellow 'sharp safe' box. Then, from inside my cargo jeans pocket, he removed my cling film wrapped stool. "What do we have here?"

"Oh," I said. "That's my shit." It too was plopped into the box, and I thought that was funny.

Paperwork was handed over a desk that was a clone of the desk sergeants at the front of the station. I watched a nurse run over to help the two struggling policemen in the cell. The female officer was friendly and Christ I needed that. It seemed as though she had seen every kind of low life scum and her own survival strategy was to be nice and just get through each day.

"Am I in prison?" I said. I was disorientated, exhausted and my heart was still racing.

"No darlin, your being detained. It's a cell. Everything will feel better in the morning."

She asked me if I wanted a blanket. I said yes. Then she offered me a pillow. I said yes. Then she asked if I wanted anything else, and I requested a coffee. She said the best she could do was water in a plastic cup. I said yes to that too. It seemed that that was all I could say. I was shown into the tiny cell, the cuffs released and the door slammed closed. Soon she returned with a plastic cup of water, and a cinnamon roll in a plastic wrapper. "We had a shoplifter in here earlier, too late to return the goods. Loads of cakes. You'd not believe the things crack heads steal. Don't tell anyone I gave you cake too you though okay?"

I nodded. The door slammed closed again and sat. Eating the pastry. The guy in the other cell was still screaming and banging on the door. The inside of my cell was so bright, the light bounced of the white tiles and I thought I might get snow blindness. I liked the policewoman, she was kind. The only kindness I'd seen in forever. I burst into tears. That full on, desperate, lost, hopeless, helpless, snot bubble cry that has your body convulsing. Turns out I was wrong

133

before. You can cry yourself to sleep. If you are as sad and broken as I was.

Morning came and once again, I'm in the same police station, at the same table in the same interview room. Breakfast would have been nice. I sat waiting for the Cuvlum and Short show like before. The only real difference was that this time I have an erection. I'm pretty confident that I took way too much Viagra, I can't believe I still have my hard-on. Have they pieced everything together yet? I can't imagine they have had enough time. Or maybe they have recognised me as the rapist. When they said they'd be watching me they really meant it. I guessed they were watching me now though. They'd held me for enough time to ensure I was hungry and cold so more compliant. Every hour I was here was an hour I couldn't get the recipe to the Thugs. The recipe for cocaine, that now is in the yellow box with the rest of my stuff. Do I just tell em everything? Let them deal with the thugs and the Ukrainian masochists? Surely though, even if I did, and the police caught them, I'd be killed by the ones they didn't catch. Things couldn't possibly be worse.

The scenario was the same. Short came in and stood. Cuvlum came in and sat quietly, sipped his coffee and thumbed through a file. It was formulaic. I thought about pointing this out but didn't think it would be well received.

"So, your a comedian then?"

Thank God he didn't say rapist. "Pardon?"

"A funny guy. A real funny guy." He sipped his coffee

134

and shuffled in his seat as if he couldn't get quite comfortable. He then shot me an angry look, "The beat off thing. I suppose you think that was funny?" I did. I thought about pointing this out but didn't think it would be well received. Detective Short was glaring at me.

"Tell me about the drugs and where you were taking them?"

"What?" I said. Nothing ever made sense with these two. It's like I kept walking in, half way through a detective movie written by Pinter. Mia liked Pinter, I never got it, there were never enough words.

"The *shit!*" he said.

"What?" I said again. I looked about as if an answer would appear in the air.

"We saw you leave a location we have had under observation for some time. So we tailed you, and we have *you* talking to an unknown accomplice about the *shit*." There was another difficult silence and Cuvlum went into a stare off. I could feel the carpet burns on my testicles were still in heal mode because every time I moved a leg I found they had glued themselves to the fabric of my jeans and painfully ripped themselves free.

"Do you have anything you'd like to say to me?" Cuvlum asked.

"Got nothing," I replied.

"Well, let me tell you what you've said to someone else," Cuvlum continued. "You said," he opened a file and read from a transcribed conversation, "And I quote, I have it. It's wrapped. I have *a big wrap of shit*."

135

Oh. My. God. They didn't know I was talking about actual shit. And how did they know what I said? So I asked. "How do you know what I said?"

"I'm glad you asked that," Cuvlum said. He shot a look at Detective Short and requested he get Detective Lorner. Moments later, detective Short returned with a very smart, young looking woman. She was very pretty, petite and with intense brown eyes that darted over me. Her face was framed by long, shiny dark brown hair that was sun kissed lighter at the ends. Though not contemptuous, she gave me a look of curiosity. Assessing me. I couldn't keep track of where she was looking, but could tell straight away that she was super smart and a league above the men in the room. Her eyes scanned my body as she analysed me, took my measure. In the corner of her mouth she was fighting back a grin, as if she knew stuff nobody else did. For whatever reason, maybe the ineptness of detectives Cuvlum and Sort, but She didn't take here eyes off me. I would class it as intrigued.

"This is Detective Lorner. SOCA," Cuvlum said.

"Oh, pleased to meet you Detective Soca," I said, and roused a smile to match her suppressed one.

She relaxed and sort of smiled back, "Its Lorner"

"Oh, sorry, hello Lorna," I said. "That's very informal, being on first names and all. Is that some kind of strategy?"

"No." she said. "Its not. I'm Detective Lorner. SOCA"

"Ohhhhh," I said. Trying to look more intelligent. "Lorna-soca. That sounds Italian. Is it Italian?"

She looked at me, still smiling, but I think I caught a trace of building irritation in her brown eyes. "Detective Lorner. SOCA. S. O. C. A." She spelled it out, "As in F.B.I., Serious, Organised, Crime Agency."

"Ahhh," I said. Any title with serious in it has to be, well, serious. If ever there was a hint to shut up, that was it. She continued. "When we retrieved your bag before, we placed a listening device in the jeans you had in there. We've been listening to everything since we returned the bag to you," she said. She smiled again and broke eye contact as she looked at the desk "We liked the fisting thing by the way, very funny."

"Thank you," I replied. I think she liked me. I hoped she liked me anyway.

This made Cuvlum visibly uncomfortable. I'm not sure if it was that she made him look stupid, that she was a woman and superior in both rank and intellect or that I made him ask me to fist him. Which ever it was, he didn't like it. He stood up and tried to regain control of the interview. "The thick granite walls of the subjects office and the noise of the clubs made recording difficult, but YOU were kind enough to discuss your *drugs business* while you were outside walking. Making it easy for *us* to *capture* audio."

Culvum had developed an odd trait. He was exaggerating odd words. It reminded me of how my mother used to scold me as a child, "What did *yooooou* do now?" But Cuvlum seemed to be stressing the wrong words and it made him sound more than a little retarded.

Cuvlem said, "The *shit*, who were you taking it to?"

"Woa, you totally have the wrong idea." I said.

"Do we? *Dude?*" Cuvlum sneered. He really was not a happy bunny. "Do we indeed." he said again, very smugly. He stood up, pressed a buzzer and left. He quickly returned with a wooden clipboard. He placed it in the middle of the table between us. On it was a clear plastic zip bag, secured with tape that had 'EVIDENCE' printed on it. There was a hand written label on the bag but it looked like a five year old had scribbled on it. Inside the plastic bag was my cling-film wrapped shit.

"Oh my God, you don't understand, that's my shit" I said.

"Come on, don't be silly *ALL* this shit is just for *YOOOUU*?" Cuvlum was standing and trying to dominate me, break me. "Who were you on the phone to then?" Cuvlum asked sounding angry. His anger seemed to stem from the fact that, even with the evidence before me, I wasn't coughing. I mean that like in telling everything not real coughing. I daren't cough for real, it would play havoc with my sticky balls. "Shall I tell you whom you were on the telephone too?" He continued, not waiting for an answer. "The person you were going to *CUT* your *SHIT* with and distribute it with. It was a dealer. And I want there name. Now!"

"NO, no, you don't understand, you literally have my shit. That's my actual shit right there."

"Do I look *STUPID* to you?" Cuvlum shouted. The sound bounced off the walls of the tiny interview room. I have to admit, that did scare me a little. "Make it easy on yourself. We were just about to test it. Save us some time and tell us what it is, it will help you too in the long run you know." Both Short and Detective Lorner seemed impressed with Cuvlum's chest beating.

"Look, I'm trying to, its shit, as in a SHIT."

Before I could stop him. Cuvlum tore open the bag. My wrapped stool thudded to the table. It was pretty solid. From his inside pocket, Cuvlum removed and opened a pen knife and violently stabbed it into my turd.

"No, no, no, no, no, no, no – you don't understand."

"SHUT IT!" Cuvlum barked as he sawed my shit in half revealing the softer inside, "Cannabis resin?" he questioned as he continued sawing. "Heroin?"

"Its shit," I said.

In a display of power and control, he slammed down the knife and sunk his finger in, scooped up a large piece, and placed it in his mouth. "You can always tell resin by..." He stopped abruptly.

Cuvlum saw me cringe, just before the taste exploded on his tongue. He was mashing his tongue on the roof of his mouth as the smell hit. He went white. Detective Lorner caught a whiff. She looked at the shit on the table, then at Cuvlum, then at me, then at my shit again, then back to Cuvlum. She cupped her hands in front of her mouth to catch vomit. She ran to the buzzer, hammered on it, and sprinted out of the room as soon as the door allowed. Cuvlum also cupped his hands over his mouth and made some primitive barking sort of urging noises. His body convulsed as it rejected the filth it had just ingested. He power vomited into his hands. Droplets of sick exploded out, spattered my face and peppered the desk. He too ran out of the room. Detective Short, excused himself more calmly. He collected my stool by sliding it back on the clip board with a pen, and left, holding it out in front of his body as if it were a bomb that could explode at any minute.

So there I sat, for about an hour. In a little room, wearing vomit freckles, reeking of sick and faeces. I inspected my torn up fingers. Massaged my aching face and worried about my damaged genitals. It feels like the helmet of my cock has snapped off. I'm pretty sure that even if Detective Lorner did like me before, she probably didn't now. I began to think that they had forgotten about me but eventually a uniformed policeman came to take a statement. I explained that I had a shit fetish, and I went to that building to swap shit with others with a shit fetish. It was all I could think of. As I had no drugs in my possession and again they had nothing to hold me for, I was released. Thank God the CD was returned, they can't have looked at it. I informed them I didn't want my shit back, that there was plenty more where that came from. The wanted poster for me had had a biro eye patch added to accompany the moustache and glasses, so that helped. 'Go graffiti guys,' I thought. I was about to leave, after autographing loads of forms, when Detective Lorner appeared. "I'm glad I caught you," she said, handing a card under the Plexiglas protection enjoyed by the desk sergeant. "Don't lose it. I have a feeling you'll need it. I can help you." I went to take the card. Lorner deliberately didn't release her grasp from the card, ensuring my attention. The smile was gone and replaced with an emotion I couldn't quite place. "Don't lose it," she said, to press the point home. Detective Lorner was very pretty. I guessed she had spent much time concealing her looks and emotions preferring a granite exterior. Maybe that was why she was in such an advanced position. But she couldn't play poker with me, her eyes were like windows. If I had to guess at the emotion I saw, it would be concern. While it felt nice to think someone cared, the brutal reality was that the concern was most likely for the case, and not for me. Concern is based on fact, else it would just be idle worry. Hence she must know something. I took the card and placed it in my pocket. I looked into her deep brown eyes and said, very sincerely, "Thank you." Her expression remained. It was a look of not expecting to see me alive again any time soon.

# 10

## More police – different shit:

We only had a few hours left. I had to get to Bulldog and make the call to the thugs. Rough thoughts for what was next was, get the CD to the thugs, get proof that I was not a rapist from Stadnyk, and then broker some kind of end to all this. I just wanted to go home, abuse the cookie jar, maybe abuse myself and sleep. I was bored of hurting. But home wasn't a good idea for obvious reasons. So far, the Red Lion pub had been a fruitful venue for plotting, drinking and snacks. I looked at my watch, it was getting to 11am. The Lion would be open for coffee and lunches. I will sit, have a coffee, collect my thoughts and when I have a plan, call Bulldog. I stood there, looking up at the grey sky, as the rain pelted my face. I wondered if it would ever stop raining and if my body would work long enough to get me to the pub.

After a soggy, aching walk, I climbed the steps up to the entrance of the Red Lion and I fell down in the usual seat behind our usual table. Our little booth in the darkest corner of the pub. I said 'Hi,' to the landlord, but this time he didn't say anything. No rapist jokes today then. He was quite surly, maybe not a morning person I thought. The pretty girl behind the bar had been replaced by a big mean looking dude. That was a disappointment. It seemed strangely busy for this time in the morning too. Quite a few guys, and all sitting near my table. There's a whole lounge of tables, why not spread out and let a broken man have some privacy?

At the bar, the barman didn't look me in the face. Instead he kept looking over to where I had been sitting. Was he looking for Bulldog? Was he a customer of Bulldogs? He looked sheepish for sure. I thought about coffee, but under the circumstances, and the need to settle nerves "A pint of larger please." He still didn't look me in the face the rude prick and said, "Will bring it over." I returned to my table and sighed in relief. I hadn't been sure I'd make it back, walking was so fucking painful. I felt like this nightmare was coming to its conclusion but I didn't want to think about it just now. I just wanted to wait for my beer and steal five minutes of relaxation. You know when you buy a chocolate bar, open it and it's shattered inside? Only the flimsy wrapper holding everything in place? That's how my body felt. That were it not for my skin, broken bits would tumble out like a child's cupboard when it has tidied its room.

I sensed movement and the big guy from behind the bar was approaching with my pint. He kind of hurried over, spilling loads. As soon as the pint was placed down, the two tables either side of me erupted, "GETDOWNONDAFLOORNOW – GETDOWNONDAFLOORNOW."

This crazed looking guy, looking like a murderous yuppie on a power trip was screaming at me and holding what looked like a little yellow toy gun. I was too exhausted to freak out. In the last few days I had been through too much, this latest drama, frankly, didn't faze me much. I just sat there calmly and said, "Stop! Stop screaming. I can't understand one word you are saying with your yelling at me like that."

"POLICE - GET ON THE FLOOR NOW!" he screamed. More men surrounded me.

I looked about the crowded lounge, full of chairs "How?" I said, "I'd have to move the table and all the chairs. There is simply not enough room."

The crazed policeman, who clearly had watched too many cop films, kicked my table away. It was all very dramatic, knocking over a load chairs as he did so. "GET ON THE FLOOR NOW – THIS IS YOUR LAST CHANCE!" then started chanting, "FLOOR NOW – FLOOR NOW – FLOOR NOW." But when he kicked the table, my pint of beer flew off and smashed as it collided with the base of an upturned chair. On the floor where he wanted me to lie, were lots of broken pieces and a large jaggy, dangerous looking broken pint glass. I picked it up, to place it on the table. So I could clear the shards from the floor and lie on the floor just as shoutey policeman requested. But he went psycho for some

144

reason. "HE'S GONE FOR THE GLASS!" he screamed. "PUT THE WEAPON DOWN – PUT THE WEAPON DOWN – LAST CHANCE!" This guy was truely mental. Way off the chart crazy. I hadn't exhibited any threatening behaviour. "Weapon? Will you, for fucks sake, calm down," I said. "I was picking it up so I can lie down like you said. And is all the shouting absolutely necessary? I'm only about a foot away from you."

"PUT - THE - WEAPON – DOWN," he screamed again. Face red and neck all vascular.

I was about to say, "Look, it isn't a weapon, its just a piece of broken glass and I really don't want to lie on it."

What I actually said was, "Loooouuunnnnngggggghh, Gaaaaaahhhnnngggggggaaaaaaahhhh Ahhahnnngh," as the crazed policeman pulled the trigger on his little yellow toy gun. A tiny dart, attached to two wires flew out from it, and imbedded itself into my chest, filling me with 50,000 volts. All I can remember is spasming uncontrollably, I saw only ceiling. I could feel me kicking away the table. Then I could see carpet, as I fell face first. Then, and not for the first time recently, I passed out.

Neither awake nor asleep, I am shepparded along what would appear to be the same corridor, in the same police station. I'm here so often these days I am starting to recall items on notice boards, where certain rooms are and even some faces. Maybe I'll get invited to the next staff party. I'm sat on an identical looking chair, again, bolted to the floor. At an identical table, bolted to the floor. Identical yet not the same. This room was slightly bigger with a mirror filling a large aperture on the wall. I waited for the show, confident that the same 'Matrix' doctrine of interview would soon start. I read the graffiti scratched into the desk 'Da police dont know shit.' Was that a double negative? I wondered. Surely it needed to be, 'The police know shit' or maybe, 'The police know nothing'. I was never good at that grammar malarky. Underneath was another line, 'The police can eat my shit.' I desperately needed a pen so I could change it to 'The police ate my shit.'

A crazy shouty Detective burst through the door. He paced up and down, arms crossed as if fighting an arctic cold. He gulped down air as if to make a huge speech but then just pointed at me. Wagging his finger. Then, as abruptly as he arrived, he left.

'What the fuck was all that about?' I thought.

In he burst again. He sat at the desk in front of me. "I am Detective Cross." How appropriate, I thought. He was clearly fighting hard to remain composed. "Do you know why you are here?"

"Because you tazered me?"

"We were smarter than you thought huh? We found you didn't we? Caught you didn't we? Didn't plan on that did you?"

"What?" I had no idea what Cross was on about. Once again, it appeared I was the only person on my page of the script. Was every policeman mental?

"C'mon, you went for the glass, wanted to fight your

146

way out didn't you? Didn't like it did you? You sick son-of-a-bitch! Not such a big man now are you? You piece of shit."

"The *glass* was on the *floor*!" I said. "I just picked it up." Detective Cross completely lost the plot,*"COME ON THEN, IF YOU FANCY YOUR CHANCES – TAKE A SHOT, COME ON! NOT SO SCARY NOW ARE YOU? YOU EVIL BASTARD. COME ON!"* Detective Cross stood, arms out in a faux crucifix, begging me to fight him. I was petrified! It looked like his bulging eyes might pop out at any moment. Everyone in the last few days has been straight up crazy. The door flew open, two policemen charged in, and grabbed Detective Cross, dragging him out while he shouted, "Get your fucking hands off of me." All the while he was reaching out to grab me. The buzzer buzzed, they dragged Cross out and the door slammed shut. Just like that. I was alone. Again. If I wasnt so exhausted, I would have tried to figure out what the hell was going on.

Moments later, Detective Cross returned. He apologised for his behaviour, saying it was unprofessional and that he should extend to me courtesy and understanding. After all, I might be ill. It might not be my fault. He sat at the table in front of me, rolled his head to release the tension, it sounded like the child safe lid on a bottle of pills. Cross then removed his tie and said, "Tell me about the rape."

To be quite honest, I was quite relieved. Maybe I could just sort this whole mess out.

"Which one, the girl by the football field or the transvestite?"

Detective Cross shut his eyes, his jaw bulged as he

clenched his teeth. His whole head went red. He hated me. I could tell. Then, after a brief moment he spoke again. "Leigh-anne Stadnyk, the *disabled*, Leigh-anne Stadnyk."

"Ooohhhh, THAT rape," I said, and laughed, because that wasn't actually a rape. In fact neither were the transvestite or the girl. Well the girl was, but it wasn't me. You know what I mean. "Ohh, I thought you meant the other rapes," I laughed again. "Yeah, that was weird," I said. Maybe it was because I laughed that Detective Cross exploded. He jumped up and yelled, *"YOU EVIL BASTARD."* He grabbed me by the hair and slammed my face into the table. The sound was awful, the noise of the impact bounced around the little room, I screamed, "Ahhhhrgh – what the fuck?"

I tried to pull the chair out to hide under the desk, but of course it was still bolted to the floor. So I ran away from Detective Cross as he chased me around the table.

The two policemen from before burst in and dragged Detective Cross away again. And just like that, once more, I was alone. More confused than ever. Detective Cross had slammed the right side of my face into the desk. The side where my lip was already split and the egg sized bruise was trying to heal. I could feel my face burning from the blood rush as other parts started to swell. If it wasn't for my throbbing face and feeling exhausted, I would have tried to figure out what the hell was going on. I know I said that just now, but this time I have a fat face and I mean it.

The buzzer sounded, Detective Cross entered again. I flinched and covered up as if expecting the ceiling to fall

148

in. I thought he would attack me this time without any discussions. "I'm sorry," he said. "I'm finding this difficult." he continued. He returned to his chair, looked over at the mirror in the wall and then back to me. He unbuttoned the top of his shirt. First the tie and now the shirt, was he planning on performing a strip tease for me? "It 's just that I, no, we, don't understand. Why disabled? Was it some sort of game?"

"Hey, don't judge me," I said. "It was what she wanted. She fantasised about it."

"What she wanted?" Detective Cross spat. Then he spat again, "What SHE wanted?" He was nodding his head like one of those nodding dogs you put in the back of cars, and mumbled, "She wanted – *SHE* wanted." Our eyes met. I could tell he was going to hurt me. He leapt up and screamed "Ahhhrrrrgh what SHE WANTED you sick fuck." He grabbed my hair again and slammed my face into the table multiple times. I was right then. In between the rhythmatic slams Detective Cross yelled, "You filled her with butter you sick fuck, you fucking filled her with butter!" All the while he was drumming my face on the table. Buzzers. The door flew open again and policemen storm in. This time there were three. They restrained Detective Cross and took him away as he clawed out at me. My eyes were still spinning in my head. Face ballooning. Brain now paté. The desk was pink wet, a fluid of my combined blood, saliva and tears. "It wasn't butter. It wasn't fucking butter," I said to the empty room.

I know that if Cross came in and gave me more shit, I would die on the spot. My body would just shut down like Rutger Hauer did in Bladerunner.

Instead I was left for a prolonged time, long enough to worry about Bulldog. All this was eating into the time I should be getting the recipe to the thugs. I was just about to drift off when the buzzer sounded and a calm and distinguished looking gentleman entered the room. He was dressed in a well worn looking linen blazer and expensive, artificially faded blue shirt. You couldn't help but conclude that all the effort to have the appearance of casual was very deliberate and had probably taken a great deal of effort. So in effect, not casual at all.

This new guy was calm, confident and relaxed. "I am Dr. Roberson," he said as he took a seat. His movements slow and precise.

"Are you here to examine my injuries?" I asked.

"No, I'm not that kind of Doctor. Do you think they need looking at?"

"Do you?"

"No."

He smiled. "I think you will be just fine. I'm a Doctor of criminal psychology and I would like to talk to you. Is that okay?" You could tell this guy was trained in attaining facts and details. He had an arsenal of open and closed questions. Asking me if it was 'okay'.

Dr. Roberson commanded your attention by using silence

well too. He removed his glasses, cleaning them with a white cotton handkerchief withdrawn from within his jacket. He inspected his glasses further before returning them to his face, then crossed his legs and gave me another smile. Woolfish. "Everyone in my profession dreams of having that one case. The one that leads to something big. A published paper, a book even. I'm actually quite excited by you." he said.

"ME?" I said.

"Yes, you," he continued. "I have so many questions. You fit some profiles but not others. You are a conundrum my friend. Quite a pickle." He mused at me for a while, making a steeple with his fingers and pressing them against his pursed lips. Looking at me as if I was some kind of prize. Then he went on, "What motivated you eh? Was it fame? Or was it voices in your head?"

"What?" I said. I thought about getting a t-shirt with 'what?' printed on it. What motivated me was a damned scary perverted Ukrainian, but I couldn't say that could I?

"Did God make you do it? We have known criminals escalate before, but you were on some kind of fast track. Young girl, transvestite, cripple."

Hang on one fucking minute, I thought I was in here for being a man whore rapist, why were they bunching the two other rapes in? I know that I'd mentioned them but they hadn't seemed that fussed before. Was she still sedated or something? "You don't understand," I said, but Dr. Roberson waved his hand and cut me off, smiling as he did in a mock 'Everything will be fine' display. "That's right,

151

I don't understand," he said. "So lets go through it piece by piece, like a puzzle." Roberson smiled again. He was disturbingly smiley.

"Okay," I said.

"Why post mortem?" he questioned.

"Why what?"

"Post mortem?" he said again.

"I'm sorry, you've lost me. I didn't post anything. What's a mortem?"

"No," Dr. Roberson fake laughed as if to appease me. "Post mortem, as in done or performed after death. Why perform the sex act on the disabled woman when she was dead? And why film it?"

WOAH - did he say dead? "Did you say dead?" I asked.

"Yes." Dr. Roberson scrutinised my reaction.

"Dead, as in dead dead? Not alive dead?"

"Yes. Dead. Deceased. Ceased to be."

"She, she was dead?"

"Yes. But you knew this didn't you. You murdered Leigh-anne Stadnyk by asphyxiation. Then performed a sex act on the body. Tell me, why film it, and what was the significance of the butter?"

I felt like I was in a vacuum. I couldn't breathe. He had said dead. She was dead. I fucked a corpse and a crippled corpse at that.

"Did the butter signify your mother? Was it the dairy content? Were you not breast fed?" Dr. Roberson kept pushing for answers.

Just when I thought I'd hit rock bottom, I didn't know that when I did, I started to dig. This was awful. I didn't just fake-rape a cripple, I actually fake-raped a dead, fat, cripple. Just thinking about it caused vomit to rush up from inside me.

Dr. Roberson continued, "Was the sex act on the corpse a way of challenging us? As it's not actual rape if she's dead. You can't rape a dead body, is that it?"

My mouth went wet and was occupied by a metallic taste, I was going to throw up. I was horrified. Disgusted. "Im gonna be sick," I said. The room seemed huge, and spinning like I was drunk or had vertigo. I'm wanted for murder now? "Wasn't me," I protested. It felt like my vomit was stuck in my throat. I held on the bolted down table so I didn't fall down, but my legs were buckling from under me.

"But we know it was you. You filmed it for us. Hell, you even took off your balaclava, smiled at the camera and saluted. You winked."

Oh God, no. I thought. Bulldog was right. That fucker Stadnyk had set me up. Dizzy, I tried to speak but couldn't find the words. Dr. Roberson reached down into his satchel and withdrew his iphone and started using it to dictate notes, "The subject is clearly in distress with the facts as presented. A text book, if rather extreme example of multiple personality disorder." He studied me briefly as if I was a great master painting, and then spoke to me like I was a five year old. "Are – you – on – any – medication?"

153

I didn't know if I was going to pass out or vomit.

"Do – you – know – where – you – are?"

Everything seemed so real. And reality felt like my skin had been peeled off, leaving me hyper sensitive. The weight of the last few days. The consequences. Going without my cocktail of speed and ketamine. Slowly I'd started to notice, to care. I'm like the opposite of Superman, I need my kryptonite. It stops me from being vulnerable to thoughts, feelings and contemplations. My teeth hurt. I'm grinding them and I can feel it. I need my ketamine, but I also needed the pain to wake me from this nightmare I was in, so I tried to crush my teeth into powder.

"Who am I talking to?" Dr. Roberson was loving this elaborate display of emotion. This was the moment his career had been waiting for. He, no they, believe I am a rapist and a murderer. I excite him. My brain is like a computer that won't boot. The words, the information, the answers, it is all in there I just can't seem to access it.

"Why kill? Was this your first kill? Was it sexual stimuli? Can you not achieve or maintain an erection unless your victim is suffering or dead?"

Not achieve an erection? I can't get rid of one! I threw up, or at least I tried. I did the empty stomach sort of silent roar. I collapsed on the floor. My guts felt like even they were disgusted with me and were trying to crawl out of me through my mouth. This is it. I'm snared. Caught. Panic tastes like chewing on aluminium foil with a mouth full of fillings. You salivate yet your mouth feels dry. Your head feels inflated like a balloon. If ever you've wanted to know what your life collapsing like a house of cards feels like, well, it feels just like that.

The buzzer sounded, and a person in the doorway called over to Dr. Roberson. In the gap through the door, I could see long brown hair and painted nails. Dr. Roberson excused himself. As he opened the door I could see Detective Cross looking concerned, and it was her. Was it her? Detective Lorner? I tried to call for help but could only dry heave. Then I could taste dust and I could see stars. My face was on the floor. Behind the door there was a heated exchange. I could hear Detective Cross arguing with others and an authorative female voice. Two policemen lifted me back to my chair. For the fourth time, the room was evacuated, leaving me in isolation, with nothing but panic and fear as companions. Time crawled forwards. So severe was the heated discussion behind the wall that, while I could not make out the words, the volume of the protests was so much that they oozed through the door so I knew that a debate was ongoing and marking the time passing. Time that was eating into the remaining opportunity to call the thugs and save Bulldog. It felt like days. I am too many different peoples puppet I thought. Stadnyk had played me like a fool so I don't feel half as bad stealing and giving up the recipe now. To add to the complexity of my hidden masters, two policemen entered the interview room. One stood by the open door, the other came up to me. I cringed. "You are free to go," he said.

"No, you are making a mistake there mate, I fuck dead cripples."

The door remained open, "Just fuck off out of here will you!" The officer barked.

No explanation, nothing. I was escorted to the rear of the station, to a parking area full of police cars and vans and I was dumped like a sack of rubbish. Why? Who the hell was pulling my strings now? I'd been framed for a murder, they had all the evidence they needed for a prosecution but I'm free. They could have fitted me up for the other rapes too, but didn't. Why? I was emersed in a confusing *shitsuation* I called it. It isn't a word, but it's the best I can do.


Nothing was making sense. Was I on some long, convoluted ketamine trip?

I checked my reflection in the window of a police car. I massaged the painful image I saw, my mashed face. It hurt. So I was awake. This was real. So what the fuck was going on?

I walked for a while, playing with the scenarios. It was like I was given a bag of random puzzle pieces and expected to complete it. But some pieces were missing and others seemed to be from different puzzles. My mind was a fog. I drifted along pavements like a leaf carried by the wind. All I knew is that my plodding along helped me process the information, but I still couldn't compute an answer.

I stopped at a bridge. A bridge I'd been over many times in cars and busses, but I'd never been intimate with it before. And that was how it felt, being there on foot. I was up close and personal with it. Feeling its cold stone surfaces and lichen clothing. The side of the wall I was on, with pavement and road, had no danger attached. The wall can only have been about four foot high. On the other side, was a huge drop to a railway line below. All the years I have crossed this bridge and I was unaware of the chasm on the side just beyond view. Scattered around the train tracks were shopping trolleys and traffic cones, anything a drunk student could toss off when they weren't tossing themselves off. The wind threw itself up from below. It had to be a sixty feet or more.

I peered over. The drop was strangely inviting, almost magnetic in it's attraction to my desperation. I could end all this nonsense and pain right here, for both me and those caught up in my wake. I climbed up, and sat on the wall, feet dangling into the abyss below. I don't think I seriously thought about jumping, but maybe I did. Playing the coward card. It's not like I would be missed, nobody would put a plaque on the bridge in my memory, "Someone insignificant did the world a favour here on such a date." It wasn't the first time I'd contemplated suicide. The first few times were to make you feel guilty Mia. I wouldn't say I was deep in thought, more like wallowing in self loathing so I didn't see the old guy, who had stopped beside me. He leant on the wall and spoke, "Thinking about it are you?"

He made me jump. Not literally of course. "No, not really."

"What you doing up there then son?" From the shopping bag in his hand, he passed me a can of beer, and took one himself. I cracked the ring-pull, chugged down a third and thought about what I'd say next. "Well, thinking about jumping I guess. I've made a real mess of things, and am in a shit load of trouble."

"Life isn't the bowl of cherries you thought eh?" he asked, taking a hit from his larger as he gazed into the distance.

"A bowl of shit more like." I replied.

"Son," he said, "You know, it all gets better in the end. If it ain't better, then you ain't at the end." With that, he necked the rest of his can and tossed it, like a sacrifice to the suicide Gods that lived under the bridge, and shuffled off through the rain.

They say wisdom comes with age. I can't believe that old dude could have gotten himself in the sort of shit I'm in right now, yet it didn't matter. What he had said was profoundly right. 'If it ain't better – you ain't at the end.' Up to this point I'd been jumping through other peoples hoops like a prissy little dog in a show. I'd been the passenger in the back seat. Now I come to think of it now though, I had broken in to the Ukrainian office so I had the recipe, I had some leverage. None of my puppet masters would have thought I had done that. I need to bring this shit to it's conclusion. With that thought came another, but this one was far more stark. There was a very real possibility that I might get killed. I was resigned to my impending demise but I felt that if getting killed along the way saved Bulldog, then it would be better than jumping off a bridge and leaving him to deal with the 'bowl of shit' on his own.

I can see the police knocking on my parents door and delivering the news; "Sorry to inform you, but your drug addicted, compulsive wanking, dead cripple-fucker of a son has died so that a drug dealer could live on." That right there is a pretty good 'Fuck you Dad!'

I find my phone, take a deep breath that hurt like buggery and dialled the thugs. The same ice chilling London twang answered the phone, "Tick tock facka. Times almost up."

"I know, I know. I have what you want."

"Good boy. Bring it to me nar. Any games an your a dead man."

"No games, I just want all of this over with."

"Been quite a nawty boi aincha? How is yaw good friend Detective Cuvlum?"

My blood froze. I felt vulnerable and it stifled my words. Even the thugs knew my every move. "How do you know about Cuvlum?" I was pushing for some signpost as to how everyone knew my movements. I needed something to make sense.

"We know everything. Where you are and what you do. If you want it to end, if you want to be safe – get me my faakin recipe."

After a brief discussion that was designed to scare the

shit out of me, which it did, I was given a location to take the disk with the recipe. I was expecting some place on the docks like on the films. So that, like on the films, I could run and dive in the water to make good my escape but I was given the address to some lock-up barns, in a remote countryside location.

"Oh, and one last thing. Come alone and change your clothes, don't wear what you have on. If I see you in those black clothes, you will be wearing your brains."

That was two last things. Says a lot about me when I am out smarted by someone so thick they cant tell the difference from one and two. I didn't think it wise to point out his error. Change my clothes? There can be only one reason for him to want me to change them. The listening device, placed by the sweet looking Detective Lorner. How the fuck did he know about that? How come everyone knew everything about everything but I knew nothing? I was feeling very dumb. So, in goes another puzzle piece back into the bag making the task even harder to figure out.

Next was to call Bulldog and hatch a plan. I'm no star poker player but I couldn't help the feeling that others were beginning to show their hand. Stadnyk had set me up for murder. I had his recipe and I can get the thugs off my back with it. If there was enough evidence I did the rapes, I'd be in the police station. Only two things that can mean then. Maybe they don't actually have quite enough evidence yet or I'm more valuable to the police by not being in custody. The police had video of me fucking asparagus legs, so I was pretty sure they had all the evidence they needed, so why was I more important to them twatting about outside? What occupied my thoughts the most though was how did the thugs know about Cuvlum?

Bulldog answered his phone. "Who is this?"

"Fuck me, not now you prick." I was annoyed. "You know who it is."

"Yeah. But in light of our current situation dude, I can't be too careful," he said. Then, "Dude, did you murder that cripple?"

"How the fuck do you know about that?" Things were feeling like the Truman show.

"You were on TV again last night. There is a national man hunt for you. They say that you are a very dangerous criminal and you are not to be approached. That you are a sexual sadist and prey on the week. They are telling old and disabled women not to answer the door to anyone."

"Bulldog," I shouted, "I was with you remember? I've been set up, like you said, Stadnyk fucking set me up. I only fucked her not fucked her up."

"Phew." Bulldog sounded his relief, "So, why not tell the police she was alive when you left?"

"Ahhh," A long pause took hold of our conversation as I tried to find the best way to explain away my dead cripple fucking, "About that, well, that's not strictly true."

"What? She was killed while you were there? You okay? Did you see the killer?"

"No, er, she wasn't killed while I was there either." Oh this was going to be hard to explain away, even to the Dog.

"She must have been killed after you left then, so that's okay, you have me as an alibi."

"Nooooooo, not killed during, while I was there or after I left."

"Well, that only leaves before?"

"Yes."

"Before?"

"YES!"

"She was dead when you got there?"

"Yes, yes she was."

"And you fucked her?" Bulldog's voice rose about two octaves higher.

"Yes Bulldog, I fucked her"

"But... but... she was..."

"Yeah, I know. Dead."

"Dude – you fucked a dead person."

"*I know*."

"That right there is fucking gross. Actually, you fucked a dead cripple, and that's worse! Did you know she was dead?"

"What the fuck man?" I shouted. "Of course I didn't know she was fuckin dead!"

"Sounds dead horny. Get it? Dead horny?"

"Yeah. Very funny"

"What was it like?"

"What was what like?"

"Fucking a dead person?"

"Buttery," I said.

"BUTTERY?"

"Well not real buttery but what the hell. I've called the thugs. We have to get the disk to them tonight. Remember I'm saving your ass right now Dog so quit taking the piss eh dude?"

"Okay," he said. "I was just corpsing around."

"That's funny. I'll give you that one mate. Look, it's complicated. The thug dudes know everything. There is a tangled plot here and I can't figure out what it is." I explained to Bulldog that it wasn't safe to talk, but promised to explain in greater detail when we met. I then sent him a text to meet me at the ASDA car park like before, and to bring a pen and paper. This time, due to my status as 'dangerous rapist and murderer' I couldn't wait inside, I'd have to take my chances and find somewhere suitable out on the road.

While waiting for Bulldog to arrive, I continued to grapple with the pieces to the puzzle and put them in their right place. I fought with what I knew to be fact, and how these facts related to each person, trying to find a connection. I sat for an age chewing over the little that I knew. I just couldn't see the answer. I could, however, see the white cloud approaching, and hear the angry car horns accompanying it, long before I could see Bulldog. Soon the smoky Toyota people carrier stopped to pick me up, belching white smoke into the street. Bleaching out the view from where it had come.

I stood up to get Bulldogs attention, and made the keep silent sign by placing my index finger over my mouth. I then did a mime of 'pen and paper'. Bulldog gave me a thumbs up, opened the back of the van and returned with his massive cannon of a pistol.

I mimed again 'NO' by an exaggerated shaking of the head. I pointed at him for 'you' and horizontally shook my fist for 'wanker'. Then mimed pen and paper again.

Bulldog silently mouthed 'Oh' then got the pen and paper.

I wrote a note. 'Need favour. I am bugged. Need you to go into store and buy supplies. Can you do that?'. I handed the pad to Bulldog.

He looked at the page. Eyebrows lifted in shock and wrote 'You were buggered?'

I took the pad, shot him a stern look. Then wrote 'bugged!' My handwriting has never been good and was worse now coz of tiredness, lack of drugs and fear.

He returned the pad with 'Oh'.

We stood there looking at each other, like actors who'd forgotten there lines. I silently gestured 'well?' and Bulldog replied with 'what?'

I grabbed the pad "Supplies!!!! Can you get them for me?'

He returned it with a 'Yes'.

I wrote again "Need a peak cap, new jeans, a t-shirt, a sharp knife like a Stanley knife and some gaffa tape'

Bulldog looked confused, he returned the pad to me 'Why do you need Jaffa Cakes?' I snatched the pad off him and wrote again, in big capitals 'GAFFA TAPE!'

"Oh" Bulldog silently mouthed again. Then he nodded 'Yes'.

On the pad I listed the sizes and what I needed and gave it to Bulldog, who took it and entered the store. Moments later he returned with two bulging bags. One with everything I needed, and the other full of snacks and nibbles including Jaffa Cakes which I thought was a nice touch.

We climbed into the Toyota, and I gave Bulldog a further note as a reminder 'Say nothing, looking for the bug'. We opened the crisps. I took the large carrier bag of clothes. Placed my hand in the bag and took out the hat, "What the fuck is this?" I wrote. Bulldog had bought a bright red cap, with 'I heart Justin Bieber' on it.

"It's a cap, you asked for a cap," he scrawled back.

"Is this the best you could do, I heart Justin Bieber?"

"Look, what does it matter, it was on sale, I'm not made of money."

"Justin fuckin Bieber though dude?"

I pulled out the jeans and they were the dark blue, cheapest, £9 jeans. The inside leg read Short 28 inches, I'd asked for a long 33 inches. I frowned at Bulldog, who retuned it with a shrug. "What? They were cheap?"

"The leg size 28 inches. That's half way up my fucking leg." I placed my hand in the bag, the bag that so far had been an utter disappointment, and took out a vomit inducing

Hawaiian style shirt, two sizes too big. "What the fuck man? What the fuck is this?"

"A shirt, you said to get a shirt, so I got you a shirt." Bulldog wrote, this time looking out the window, not taking the criticism well. I guess a written criticism is somehow worse than a spoken one.

"T-shirt, I said get a t-shirt. I even wrote it the fuck down, look," I angrily turned back some pages and tapped the pad, "T, fucking, shirt." The pattern on this one was so savage, anyone with epilepsy would have an instant seizure. "You got me a stupid fucking hat, jeans that would fit a midget and a ridiculous fucking Hawiian shirt. Do you hate me, is that it?"

"I'm not Gok fucking Wan, I'm not your personal bloody stylist you ungrateful prick, at least you got some free shit."

"I never said you had to pay for the stuff did I? I just asked if you would get it. I'd have given you some cash if you hadn't stormed off."

"Then why didn't you get it your self?" Bulldog scribbled.

"BECAUSE I'M A WANTED FUCKING RAPIST!"

A family pushing a trolly, stared at us through the window of the Toyota. We must have looked like two crazy guys, one beat up, tossing a notepad back and forth and silently shouting at each other.

I changed clothes. It felt good to be in something clean without dried blood or vomit, even if I did look like an idiot. As I pulled up the jeans I could see the tender tip on my cock, all abraded, and the two large weeping sores on my testicles. A guys trophy and tanks never look good, but red raw and swollen? It looked gross, like a couple of pounds of fresh turkey giblets. I stepped out of the Toyota in my ill fitting shirt, too short jeans and stupid 'I heart Justin Bieber' cap. I looked like a retard that had just got off the Sunshine Variety Bus.

All I needed to complete the look was a Balloon on a string and a big lollypop. Bulldog tried to not look, but when he did he couldn't help but burst out laughing.

Embarrassed by my appearance, I climbed back in the Toyota and set about searching for the listening device. I searched the pockets of my still warm rapist jeans. Nothing, then the hem, nothing. I turned the t-shirt inside out and there was nothing their either. But the lovely Lorner had said jeans so I returned my attention to them. All the stitching was intact, and they hadn't had the time to cut and sew. Then I saw it. Taped under the flap of one of the button down pockets. A place you'd never look, was a small round disk battery, like a slim watch battery, a tiny ribbon cable and what looked like a chip with a tiny disk shaped microphone attached. All together it was no bigger than a coin, secured in place with a strong adhesive fabric tape. Bulldog's eyes widened as I discovered it. So far the transmission would only have recorded the rustling of crisp packets, munching and maybe a little bit of shouting.

With the knife, I tried to lift of the fabric tape. But the ribbon cable looked very fragile. So, using the knife again,

167

I delicately cut away the fabric leaving the device and tape attached to a patch. Then I tore a strip of Gaffa tape and secured the bug to the inside of the cap. I threw the cap on the back seat, and beckoned Bulldog to follow me.

When far enough away in the car park on a bench reserved for the elderly and disabled, I explained the situation to the Dog. Once I had outlined things as I saw them, the gravity of the mess and the danger we were in, we both sat there in silence. Percolating. Then it was decided. Bulldog would drive me to the meeting point now. We'd get there early to scope out the location and let the smoke cloud from the Toyota disappear. Get a feel for the place. Bulldog would lie low in the car and wait for me. If I didn't reappear after two hours, he would call the police. When we got back to the car, I looped the buckle fastening of the cap around the rear windscreen wiper to keep the bugged cap outside, ensuring our privacy as we travelled. Anyone behind us would think we were Justin Bieber fans but hey, it's a little better than being thought of as a raper of fat cripples isn't it?

It was getting dark, and cold. Bulldog and I, in the shitty Toyota, made our way to make our delivery. It took us a while to find the place. Every now and then we had to double back on ourselves and when we did, we had to crawl through our own thick white smoke.

We came to a cross-roads, took the little lane opposite, and, as was described, climbed up a long hill. We past gates with stables and horses, nice. Further along the road it felt very remote. Lush grass and trees were superseded by shrub and hardy moorland grass. There was nowhere to go wrong. This road lead only ahead or back the way we came. Ahead we went. Eventually there was a clearing where vehicles had been turning, and up ahead in the distance stood a barn. It was surrounded by razor wire. It had wooden walls, and the front was inset with three large roller shutter doors. You couldn't mistake the fortified building as anything innocent or agricultural. We were miles from civilisation. I checked my phone and unbelievably I had a signal. I told Bulldog to check his so he could call the police if he needed to. His phone had too had a full signal.

I had no idea how this was going to go down. Maybe you run out of nervousness because I was oddly calm. Maybe, subconsciously I was resigned to the finality of all this and the likelihood of death. Or maybe I was just too exhausted, in too much pain and too hungry to give a fuck. I looked a mess. All bruised and swollen welts. From the blisters on my feet, my weeping sore testicles, sore bell end, pink eye, fat lip I was a wreck and I sported body colours to rival my loud shirt, all purples and yellows. If I were a wild animal, you'd have killed me just to put me out of my misery. And a misery I was. I retrieved the disk from my jeans pocket. It didn't feel like it would save my life and turn this mess around but it was all I had. I was about to get out and scope the area. No idea what I was going to look for, maybe mines, trip wires or snipers. It just seemed the proper thing to do in situations like this. I got out, took the Justin Bieber hat off the rear wiper and walked towards the barn in the distance.

My phone buzzed, then rang. I hit answer and put it to my ear, "Hello?"

"Early bird gets da worm." The bone chilling sound of one of the thugs.

"Wh.. what?" I asked.

"Your early. I like that you took the initiative to save me some time. Don't keep us waitin any longer Alice, bring me my recipe." In the distance, one of the roller shutters clacked open. Up ahead, as the entrance grew wider, the barn looked like it had a big open mouth, with a guy standing in it. Waiting for me. The voice continued, "You alone?"

I shut my eyes and clenched my teeth. How much did he know? The Toyota people carrier was a fair way back and arrived masked in smoke. It had three rows of seats and Bulldog was lying down across the middle. Out of sight. I chanced it. "Yes. I did what you said."

"Good boy," he said. "Now, walk over to the nice man you can see in the doorway."

I fondled Justin Bieber's opening to check the bug then placed the cap on my head and made my way over to the building.

As I approached, the guy in the door seemed huge. "Don't say a fucking word. Jeez what the fuck have you come dressed as? A paedophile?" I opened my mouth to respond, but got barked at with, "Shut the fuck up, did I tell you to talk?" I didn't know if this was a trick question, because he told me to not talk, but then asked me to confirm I wasn't to talk. I thought about saying 'No', but keeping my mouth shut seemed the best option. He walked over , squinting against the glare of my shirt as he lifted it to check for wires. He told me to turn around, and again checked my back and arse. I waited for him to take my cap and check that too. I was banking on my incompetence so far to provide a less thorough investigation. If he made me take off my cap, the bright sliver gaffa tape and bodged bug transfer would be blatantly obvious. Dead I would be. But he didn't. "Clean," he shouted. Then with his bunch of bananas sized hand he grabbed me by the neck, crushing it a bit and escorted me inside the barn.

I counted four men. The two from before, and two others. A wallpaper pasting table stood with a laptop on it. The laptop had a mobile broadband key in it.

As my eyes adjusted to the dark, I could see that the men were heavily armed. The two I recognised were the ones who kicked me around the Chemist's flat like an old sack of washing. The older of the two, gestured with his gun to a chair and yelled, "Sit!" I felt like pissing myself with fear like a scolded dog but did as I was told.

The younger of the two stood uncomfortably close, it

was a bit intimate. I could smell him. Like the others, he was holding a gun. What struck me was how casual they were while holding their weapons. It was particularly chilling because it was abundantly clear that they had used them many times. Unlike me, who would be rigid armed while holding a pistol, or keeping it pointing forward as I walked, like a kid playing, these guys held their guns like it was natural, something benign, like a calculator. I sat on the folding chair. I hate folding chairs, for the very fact they fold. I have seen too many clip shows on TV of people collapsing in folding chairs. To me they present as much danger as the guys with guns. This was a nightmare, one of the two of the things I fear most, folding chairs. The only things I know I'm scared of is clowns and folding chairs, outside of obvious things like guns that scare everyone. Especially when pointed at your face. I'm half expecting Pennywise the clown to turn up and complete the nightmare.

The goon next to me held out his hand, and I gave him the CD. He threw it to the older thug, who caught and placed it into the laptop. His complexion changed to blue as the computer was brought from sleep and chimed to life. There were fingered taps and clicks. A grin, then a frown. Then a deeper frown. An angry frown. 'Oh shit'. I thought.

"What the faak is dis?" he asked.

"Uh…" What could I say? I hadn't checked the files. I had to try and bluff. "It's what you asked for."

"It has a faakin encryption code on it. I can't make it out you cunt."

The guy beside me grabbed my hair and pulled my head so I was upright in the chair and focused. It felt like my head might come off.

"I'm not the…" I was about to throw myself at their mercy, explain that I wasn't the Chemist and what I'd been through to get there disk, but was silenced by a phone buzzing. The phone was made louder because it sat on the table. The thug shot it a concerned look. Then that look travelled to me. He picked up the phone and answered it. "Yes Boss?"

Boss? I had convinced myself that this guy was at the top of his food chain. However, I didn't have any time to think on it further. "FUCK," he shouted. "He's live, he's still transmitting! He's wearing a fucking wire. You little cunt." Then he said words I really didn't need to hear. "Kill him."

"WAIT," I said. But the thug beside me lifted his gun. And pointed it directly at my face. Panic hit me like an injection of fear direct to the brain. "WAIT!" The gun was compact and square. It's matte black metal only tarnished at the exit of the barrel where it exhibited some use. I could hear the laptop snap closed. I couldn't talk my way out of this. I was going to die. This was how I was going to fucking die. Fuck you Dad! I was glad my life didn't flash before my eyes, because the show would have a bit of a disappointment. Filled with beat the fan wanking games and katamine coma's as the big powerful hand trained the

173

pistol at my face. I shut my eyes and hoped it wouldn't hurt. There was a deep thunk sound and something warm spattered my face. Had I been shot? Wasn't I meant to be able to feel it? I opened one eye and most of the hand that had been holding the gun had been ripped away. A fleshy clump, everything but a thumb and a little finger was missing. Blood was gushing. He screamed. I just sat there, confused. I think I was in shock. The remaining three men looked shocked too. Then bullets started to punch holes through the walls and tore chunks out of the floor. Two rounds thudded into the handless thug, one exploded his neck, it made a bright red explosion and deformed his throat as it exited.

A vehicle skidded up outside. It was followed by more gunfire. The three thugs inside didn't seem to exhibit any emotion for their fallen colleague or any fear. I sat in my best Forrest Gump mode, amazed at what was taking place. The men inside the barn opened flight cases, retrieved automatic machine guns and returned fire. Fragments of concrete sprayed over me as more rounds smashed into the floor and bit huge chunks out of the flimsy table. I think they were aiming at me too. I 'm pretty sure the bullets that took the guys hand and neck were meant for me. I knew I should have checked for snipers. Damn it. Had I not learned anything from the shoot em up films?

I ran toward the open door. Bullets were flying everywhere. I took cover behind one of the brick walls beside the entrance.

It's not like on the films you know. The gunfire was relatively quiet, the nerve shredding noise came from the bullets tearing and smashing through what ever they were faced with. Shrapnel flys off and hits what ever is close by. Tortured metal gets torn, objects gets thrown about. It is a loud percussion of destruction. It is what you would imagine death to sound like. I soon found out that also, unlike on the films, brick walls do not provide cover. Bullets punched holes through where I was hiding, dusting me with powder. Beams of light from the car outside blazed through the holes like miniature searchlights. The smell of dust and the gases from the exploding gunfire filled my nostrils.

Volleys of gunfire were returned, with a mechanical 'cut-cut-cut-cut.' I could hear each 'cut' thudding into metal. Then a blood curdling scream from out side, as more bullets rained in overhead. The older of the remaining thugs called out, "Stadnyk's men. Go, go, go." The men employed what appeared a well rehearsed exit strategy. Me? I just ran like fuck outside! My strategy was to zig-zag as I ran and every now and then zag twice to throw off any shooters. I sprinted as fast as my blistered foot and damaged genitals would allow. I looked ahead and made for the hedge that lined the road. I could hear 'ffut' sounds as bullets missed me and buried themselves in the earth nearby. I could hear, "Get him!" and I knew that I was the 'him' . I hoped that the fire fight behind me would keep my assailant pinned down.

Up ahead, Bulldog's Toyota. Bulldog! I hoped he was okay. I imagined the car peppered with bullet holes. I ran up and it looked fine. I tried the sliding side door. It was locked! Then Bulldog sat up, wearing his ipod and looking all sleepy eyed. He'd drifted off to fuckin sleep. On seeing me, his eyes went as wide as saucers. I had no time to explain. I could see the keys were still in the ignition. I pulled the drivers door and it opened. I dived in and turned the keys. The Toyota thrummed into life. "Woa, what the fuck do you think you are doing dude and why is there blood all over your face?"

I hadn't realised how tiny Bulldog was. I could hardly fit behind the wheel.

I hit the accelerator but the Toyota didn't move. I looked down and there was no gear leaver "WHERE ARE THE GEARS – WHERE ARE THE FUCKING GEARS?"

"Your not driving my car." Bulldog shouted.

"GEARS, GEARS?"

"No way, your not insured!"

"BULLDOG, where's the fucking gears?"

"No way," he said again. "Your not insured!" As he said it, two bullets made deep 'thank' sounds as they punched into the Toyota. A third destroyed the rear window, tore through the front seat and sank a big hole in the dashboard. It showering us with diamonds of broken glass. "Ahhhhhhhrrgh," Bulldog was screaming, or it might have been me.

"On the steering wheel. It's a column," Bulldog yelled. I

could now see the gear selector. I pulled it to Drive, floored the accelerator and the golden Toyota lurched forward. Foot planted to the floor, the revs screamed, then it dumped to second, and slowly the revs climbed to a scream again. Not the best get-away car. I've seen oak trees grow faster. Two golden circles quickly approached from behind, the headlights of a car in pursuit. "DRIVE." Bulldog was hysterical. "DRIVE."

"I fucking am!" I yelled. The headlights behind grew brighter, then a car slammed into the back of the Toyota. Well, the carrier handled like a shopping trolley at the best of times, but when hit from behind, it was impossible to keep it in a straight line A grinding and scraping noise filled the air as the outside of the car deformed against a hedge. "Shoot em!" I shouted as the tires screamed when the car hit us again. I looked over to see Bulldog and all I could see was his feet. He had rolled over. "What?"

"Your gun, that fucking blunderbuss or what ever its called, fucking shoot em Dog."

Bulldog climbed from the middle to the back seat, and grabbed his giant pistol. He held it out of the broken window. There was an almighty bang as a bullet exploded out of the gun. The power of the gun's recoil ripped it free from Bulldogs hand and it bounced on the floor. He scrambled around for it amongst the shattered glass and debris. The car behind charged at us again. Bulldog lifted the gun to take aim, and let off another shot. Another huge bang, but this time it hit. One of the headlights disappeared and the chasing car violently veered to the right. It didn't stop them much though, the Toyota was playing fair and letting its playmate straighten itself out and start chasing again.

It was at this point the old Toyota took on an almost magical James Bond quality. The Smoke. As the revs picked up, the faulty turbo seal started throwing oil down the exhaust manifold. A cloud. A dense white cloud. Nothing could see through it. We flew along the country lane, bouncing about, the persuing headlight grew smaller and smaller until it became a distant glow. Through all the wind of the open rear I could still hear gunfire, so I kept my foot planted on the accelerator. The Toyota lolloped and wallowed along the lane.

I didn't want to stop. "Have we lost them? This smoke is fantastic! I love this smoke man!" I was laughing like a loon.

"Don't know," Bulldog shouted. He rested the gun on the back of the middle seat and leaned out of the broken window, scrutinising the night, trying to peer through the cloud. Travelling at speed, every divot in the road felt like a trench. "I'm not sure, but I think we've lost em," he said. Just then I hit a big pot hole. The vehicle bottomed out and it was followed by a massive bang. A bullet flew out of the antique gun and tore a chunk out of my ear before it smashed the rear view mirror then left a hole in the windscreen. Surrounding the hole was a spiders web of shattered glass. The crashing of the bottom of the car on the road had made Bulldog accidently fire his gun. "Ahhh fuck. You've shot me again you cunt. Fuck me mate, you've shot me fuckin twice! "

"Dude," he said, "I'm sorry dude."

I grabbed my ear. It was gushing blood. I was amazed I had any blood left. "How bad does it look Dog?"

"Okay I think. It's just the mirror and the windscreen."

"Not the car you fucking idiot, my ear, my fucking ear!"

"Oh. You've a piece missing. About the size of a twenty pee."

Wind was whistling in through the hole in the windscreen and I couldn't see a thing. My view was totally obscured by the cracked glass. My knees were splayed out and crushed by the dashboard due to Bulldogs tiny seating position. My balls were crushed by the tightened crotch of my £9 jeans. I really had to move the seat back but I couldn't risk slowing down. I reached down between my legs to find the lever that would let me slide it back. My fingers located a spring loaded metal bar. I pulled it and pushed with my spare breaking foot to slide the seat back. It didn't move. So I pulled harder on the bar and pushed back again. The seat still didn't slide back. So I pulled on the metal bar harder, bracing my knees against the dashboard. The steering wheel dug into my already sore crotch, mashing my carpet burned balls. I pushed with all my might to slide the seat back. As it turns out, to slide the seat back and forth on Bulldog's Toyota you need to pull a lever on the side of the seat, next to the door. The bar I was pulling was there to flip the entire seat over onto its back to gain access to the car battery below the chair. So, there I was pulling on the bar and rocking violently, using my weight and momentum to get the seat to slide backwards. The next thing I knew, I was in the back seat, facing upwards, legs round my ears, looking up at Bulldog. The empty seat flipped back and the now driverless Toyota careered down the country lane. A severed finger rolled out of my shirt pocket, travelled across my chest and came to a halt at the base of my neck. Bulldog looked at it and screamed, "Ahhhh it's a finger, get it away!" Of course, I didn't know it was a finger. What he was screaming made no sense. I grabbed the bloody digit. Looked at it, realised it was the gunman's finger, then we both screamed.

I tried to throw the finger out of the shattered windscreen as Bulldog scrambled for the steering wheel but the finger bounced off the ceiling and landed in Bulldogs open mouth. Bulldog shrieked and spat the finger out. "It went in my mouth, in my fucking MOUTH!" He cried. Just then the car bounded off a hedge, throwing Bulldog on top of me. I pushed him off and tried to grab the steering wheel myself. The speed of the Toyota was still enough to have us tossed around like ragdolls. The car ricocheted off a bank and threw me back. I accidently sat on Bulldogs face. The view outside was obscured by shattered glass, but not enough to hide the tight right angle bend we were speeding towards. Even though there was no foot on the accelerator, we were rolling down hill and picking up speed. I tried to steady myself to dive for the wheel as Bulldog tried to escape from under my ass. I dived forward and got one hand on the wheel. I was about to use it pull myself back on the seat and regain control, when the back of the Toyota swung around and smashed off another hedge. I bounced in the air and landed on my back in the front passenger seat still holding the wheel.

The view was clearer through the hole in the passenger side of the windscreen. I sat up just in time to see only sky as the Toyota left the road, punching through a long leafy hedge Dukes of Hazzard style. For a split second we were airborne. I looked and screamed. I looked at Bulldog and he screamed too. The car crashed down, throwing us and all the crap in it through the air like we were in Dorothy's tornado. We were showered with crisp packets, broken glass and empty drink cans. As we landed I was thrust into the foot well. I now knew how those circus girls feel when they are stuck in their bottles. The vehicle rolled on for a while with a loud rushing sound as it mowed down the crops in the field we had landed in. Then we stopped. I unfolded myself, managing to get enough of myself out to kill the engine. "What the fuck are you doing?" Bulldog yelled.

"I don't want the car giving us away with its smoke if we are stuck here mate. This could be quite lucky, we are off the road and the fuckers will still be after us."

"Okay, okay, good idea." Bulldog was hyperventilating.

Deformed by impact, the passenger door whined and

creaked as I pushed it open. Broken glass spilled out as I stepped into the darkness. It was eerily quiet. Bulldog joined me outside. We looked back to where we'd come. The full moonlight was enough to highlight the smoke from the Toyota. For as far as we could see, a thick white fog blanketed the fields. It was a good few minutes before, way off in the distance, two speeding cars could be heard. Then we heard nothing but wind and the far off thrum of a distant car.

We sat there, not speaking, for over an hour to ensure we were no longer pursued. I slid open the side door and retrieved some crisps from the bag of food that was now strewn all over the interior and sat down. Bulldog also took a bag and sat beside me. "Well," I said, as I stared into the distance, "Fuck a duck."

"Fuck – a – duck." Bulldog agreed, through a mouth full of crisps, spraying chewed food. We sat and said nothing, just eating the crisps. This was too much for us to fully comprehend. "Saw someone killed today," I said to break the silence.

"Your kidding?"

"Nope," I replied. "Had his hand shot off, then the guy took one in the neck"

"Was that his finger?"

"I guess."

"Fuck dude, your lucky to be alive."

"Pretty much. Was fucking horrible and petrifying at the same time."

"So what happened in there?"

"Fucked if I know." I thought for a second, chewing a crisp, then told him my view of the events. "I sat down and they took the disk. But the disk was encrypted so they couldn't read it. Then, some guy rang and told them I was still bugged, so there must have been another guy with a scanner or something. Then, this big cunt was about to shoot me in the face and Stadnyk turned up. Or at least some of his men turned up. I assume to get me for stealing the recipe."

"Fuck, your kidding?"

"Nope. Then all hell broke loose, fucking guns and bullets everywhere. Funny thing though, Stadnyk turning up to kill me probably saved my life."

We both sat and tried to digest the situation and the crisps. "C'mon I said, lets get out of here."

We both stood and swept our bodies free of crisp dust and broken glass. Bulldog has tuned out to be a solid friend. When this mess is behind us, I'm going to make time to get to know him better. So far, in my shitty life, a near stranger is the only person to have not let me down.

Dog flipped the drivers seat back into place, jumped in and fired up the engine. It started on the first turn, he looked at me wiggled his eyebrows and said "Toyota's dude, most reliable cars in the word.". I jumped in and kicked out the rest of the windscreen. Bulldog put the car into 'drive' and stepped on the accelerator . The wheels just spun on the spot. He tried again but to no avail. We were stuck. I got out. The wheels were bogged down in the soft soil. "I'll push," I said. "You gas it." Bulldog buried his foot to the floor and I pushed from behind. The wheels spun, throwing mud, but the Toyota was too heavy. Each time I pushed, the wheels almost freed themselves, but it just wasn't enough. The wheels slid back into the trench.

Bulldog got out and took a look. "Fuck me. Look at the bullet holes!"

There were three deep finger sized holes in the dented panels.

"I know," I said. "The wheels are stuck. The ground is hard enough, if I can push it out a bit more but its too heavy."

Bulldog snapped his fingers. "Have an idea," he said, then ran off into the darkness.

He was gone a while so I had another bag of crisps. Eventually he returned, with a big rock in his arms. "What if we both push?" he said.

"Yeah, I guess that might do it."

Bulldog started the Toyota, put it in drive and spun up the wheels. Then he placed the large boulder on the accelerator pedal. The engine screamed, spewing more white smoke as the wheels tore into the earth, raining grit and earth against our legs. I pushed, and quickly Bulldog ran to the back and pushed with me.

"You GENIUS!" I shouted as I heaved.

The revs dropped temporarily as the cars wheels were almost free, but they slipped back down. We pushed harder, and this time the tires bit into the soil at the top of the ditch, gaining traction and drive. The Toyota was free at last, and it sprinted away. By itself.

I might have been a bit hasty with the term genius I thought as we both stood there, watching the car drive itself away from us as fast as it could, the rock planting the accelerator to the floor. We could hear the fucking thing going through the gears on its own as it picked up speed. It threw crops in its wake like a speed boat going through water as it ploughed on and disappeared into the black distance. Seconds later there was a crash, one last scream of engine noise and then silence. We said nothing, just looked at each other. We followed the Toyota wide road of flattened crops. Almost perfectly straight but for the odd deviation, the lane of crushed vegetation lead us toward the sound of the impact into the last of the white smoke.

Bulldogs poor Toyota, with its bullet holes and smashed windows now had a fucked up face that looked almost as bad as mine. The front was concertinerd up. A sliding door on its side, beside the car. Bits of trim hanging off. Twisted metal looking all angry and sharp. The car was as dead as I should be. Then, it started to rain. Thick droplets of rain fell, drumming off the carcass of the dead people carrier. There would have been the nice smell of fresh rain were it not for the stink of rusty steam escaping from the smashed radiator and dirty oil like blood spilling form the wreck of the Toyota. I wondered if the bug would be ruined if my cap got wet, and was about to take shelter inside what was left of the people carrier. The bug! I had an idea.

I was tired of running, of being other peoples puppet. Tired of trying to work out what the fuck was going on. Clearly I wasn't smart enough to fit the pieces together. But then, I was never good at solving puzzles. I needed to bring the whole situation to the attention of someone who could. Bring events to a close.

"Bulldog," I said "Don't worry, but I'm going to call the police." Bulldog was about to protest. I stopped him. "Bulldog, they just tried to kill me, and they think I'm you. So long way around, you should be dead right now. We are in no position to handle this by ourselves dude. These people are killers. We have the Ukrainian Mafia AND some London mobsters after us."

"I'm scared dude," he said, as he sat, knees together like a frightened child. I checked my phone. No signal.

"I know dude," I said. "Me too. Don't worry, just wait here till the cops come for you. You'll be a lot safer if you stay here."

"What are you going to do?"

"I'm not absolutely sure. But a wise man once said 'It gets better in the end and if it ain't better, you ain't at the end.' He was right. I need to bring this crazy mess to a close."

"How ? You can't just roll up without at least some kind of plan."

"I will think of something. I have an idea, just I've not worked out the details yet."

"What the fuck, you cant just, I mean, fuck." Bulldog got up and paced through the rain, ran his fingers over his shaved head in frustration and then yelled, "FUCK."

"It's okay."

"No. It's far from fuckin okay. Stay. Call the Police and wait here with me, we can sort this shit out with them."

"This isn't going to stop Bulldog, don't you get that? We will never be safe, things will never be normal unless I end this shit. I'm going to see Stadnyk. I have a feeling it all ends with him."

"Dude – for fucks sake, he's framed you for murder and he just tried to kill you. You go see Stadnyk, you will die."

I paused before what I said next. I couldn't believe I was saying it or that I actually meant it. And I did mean it. "Better one of us dead than both of us. I think I worked out a while ago that I wasn't going to make it out of this mess. At least I get to choose how."

"Dude…" Bulldog said, and then looked like he was about to cry.

"Don't worry. I'll be fine. Just wait here for the cops okay?"

Bulldog nodded then covered his face with his hands.

"I've gotta go," I said. I love ya man is what I should have said.

Bulldog nodded, wiped his nose on his sleeve and stood. We hugged, and I wondered if I would ever see him again. I was too emotional to talk, so I just walked away.

187

# 11

## Playing your hand with all your fingers.

I am a shit poker player. Really I am. I don't understand the rules and I have a 'tell'. I can't bluff and can't work out if others are bluffing. But in a game, I usually win at least one hand before I lose everything I have. In this game I've been forced into, statistically, I can't keep coming up short. It was time to call for a new pack of cards. It was time for one last throw of the proverbial dice and hope for the best.

I walked through the fields to keep off the road, just in case the thugs were still looking for me and headed for the orange glow of the distant city. I kept checking my phone for a signal. Eventually the fields yielded to an industrial estate, and beyond that, a housing estate full of row after row of identical houses. I had a vague idea where I was. Everything painted orange by streetlight gave an eerie cartoon feel to the deserted streets I was walking along but I recognised them. I checked my phone again and this time had a signal. I called the police and told the operator I needed to speak to Detective Lorner from SOCA urgently.

The operator tried to get details from me and go through a system they were trained to do. It reminded me of our scripts at Colorpure. "No," I said. "This is a matter of life and death. I can give Detective Lorner what she wants. I can get her everything, but I will talk only to her." I was told to hold. Then told to be patient. Then told Detective Lorner wasn't answering her phone. "Try again please," I said, politely. The operator said it was just an answer phone. "Patch me through to her mobile then," I demanded.

"We can't do that, this isn't like on television."

"Look, people will die tonight. I will probably die tonight. Have you a record of this number?"

"Yes, sir." The operator said, then continued, "Sir, I must insist."

"LISTEN!" I said to demand her attention. "Put me through to her answer phone but before you do, write this down. I am going to Stadnyk, he tried to kill me because of a secret cocaine recipe. I am going there now. Did you get that?"

"Yes sir."

"Do everything you can to contact Detective Lorner at SOCA and get her that message. My life is in your hands. Now, put me through to her answer phone. Please."

"Okay sir. I can send you her mobile number by text maybe."

"Oh, one more thing. My friend, name of Bulldog needs to be rescued. The people who are trying to kill me will eventually find him. He had nothing to do with any of this, make sure you tell Lorner that." I relayed the directions to where Bulldog was and gave her Bulldogs mobile number so they could maybe try and trace it. It was in or near the car somewhere for sure.

A short ring tone and I was through to Lorner's answer phone.

"This is Detective Lorner of the Serious Organised Crime Agency. I am sorry but I can't take your call right now but if you leave your name, a contact number and your crime reference number or the nature of your enquiry, I will return your call at my earliest convenience." Her voice was all sensual and husky. Under any other circumstance, I would have used her voice to wank to. Then there was a beep for me to leave a message, but I hadn't thought what to say. So I just babbled, "They knew about the bug. They know everything. They even knew about Cuvlum. They tried to kill me. Stadnyk tried to kill me. People got shot and killed. I found your bug, and have put it in my Justin Bieber, hat. I'm going to see Stadnyk now. I pray you get this and the bug works." I hung up. I was about to make another call when my mobile beeped. A text. Detective Lorner's mobile number.

I rang the number and it went straight through to her answer phone. I thought about what to say this time. It was late, she's probably in bed with a stunning, buff and successful husband and wouldn't get this till the morning. I'd most likely be dead by then. So before I hung up I said, "Look it's me again, one more thing, I will probably be dead by the time you get this, but check what the bug records,

I will try to get everything. Also, you are very pretty and I'd love to fuck you. Bye." Then I killed the connection.

I was going to confront Stadnyk. I would find out, once and for all, what was going on or this would never end. Everything was tangled together.

I slid open my phone, found Stadnyk's number and called it.

Stadnyk answered, but before he could draw a breath to speak, I said, "You fucking set me up you bastard. You framed me for the murder of your wife."

"Yes. But resilient you are yes?"

"And, AND you tried to kill me tonight."

"No, no, not at all. No try kill you. Just business. It how we do things. You can't get a solicitor to take rival drug lords to court for stealing your intellectual property yes?"

"We need to talk."

"We do?"

"Yes, we do. I want to end this. I have information. I want my freedom back. I don't want to be looking over my shoulder every day. I'm coming to see you now," I said.

"Where are you, we look for you. We peak you up."

"No," I said. "I will come to you. Meet me at your office." But then Cuvlum's words tumbled out of my memory. *'We couldn't hear because of the granite walls.'* The bug in my cap probably wouldn't work. I'd fucked up again. But then I had another idea.

"Wait," I said. "Maybe picking me up is a good idea, it might be easier." I ran to the entrance of the industrial estate. Beside a large building, I read the street name and relayed it. "I'm on Eagle Way, in front of a company called Mediplax."

"I get you in five minutes, we talk yes?"

"Yes."


Five minutes flew past. I needed more time to compose myself and find the right questions to get the answers I needed. I didn't have that luxury. The limousine arrived almost instantly. The door opened and Stadnyk sat alone inside in the back. Mr Enormous was driving. Now, here was the advantage to having an old shit phone. Unlike the modern smart phones that need an area big enough to accommodate a touch screen. My old phone was compact and small. Better yet, the illuminated screen goes dark seconds after you make a call. I slid the phone open with one hand and pressed redial. I heard Detective Lorner's answer phone message and turned the volume down by keeping my finger on the side button.

"No funny business, just talk okay?"

"Get in, we talk."

I climbed inside, hiding the phone by placing it behind me on the seat ensuring Lorner's answer phone would record every detail. Stadnyk poured himself and me a shot of Vodka, from an elaborate decanter. What is it with all the fancy bottle?. He threw back the shot. I did the same. The liquid instantly warmed the back of my throat.

"Why you dressed like special person?" Stadnyk asked.

"That's not important right now. Why did you set me up?"

"You know," Stadnyk looked into his glass, refreshed it with more vodka, "I like you. You survivor, this I like."

"Why then? Why not just kill her like you did and leave it. Why fit me up?"

"Wife think I try kill her before. This why she in wheelchair. She has much information on me. Blackmail me. She cost me millions each year. But with you, a rapist, make it easy to get rid her and take heat off."

"Hence the elaborate rouse."

"What this mean?" Stadnyk asked.

"The balaclava, camera, for me to take the mask off and look into camera, so I would catch the blame. The whole thing was staged. So who did kill her?"

"I kill that bitch. I do myself. Want to see the life snuff out of that cow."

"And I take the fall."

"This is right."

"So why did you try to kill me tonight?"

"Not me, my men. I did not send to kill you, I send to kill everyone. You just there."

"Why though?"

"They after my business. I have reputation to protect, a market to control. Besides, they had my secret cocaine recipe."

Panic started to seep in. How did Stadnyk know they had the recipe? I had only just delivered it. I had to find out how much he knew. I had to ask. "How do you know they had your recipe for the cocaine?"

"Because you give to them."

FUCK. Once again, everyone else knew everything. How the hell did he know? While trying to set a trap, I had accidently walked into one myself. I had handed myself over to the man who would kill me. Stadnyk threw back the vodka, poured another and gestured an offer to me for another. I declined.

"Tell me," he said. "I see you many time in my casino. Play poker sometimes but sometimes tables. You know what fish is?"

Oh no, I thought, here we go again, guess the meaning. Jews, horse now fish? "Fish, as in the sea, cod, trout, finny fish?".

"No, not quite." Stadnyk pondered for a second before he continued, "Is gambling term. A bit like whale. You know what whale means?"

"I've heard of it, but I don't really know what it means," I said.

"I explain," Stadnyk replied. "A whale, is big fish, a high roller. Someone important, with money, you understand?"

"Yes."

"Well a whale can also be your business, your big clients yes?"

"Yes, I can see."

"Problem is, there is also sharks. These bad. You need to kill shark to protect your whales, you see?"

"Kind of."

"But you need to know where the sharks are to kill them. Every ocean has sharks, but must find them yes? So you send out bait. You send out a fish. Sharks are predators and you send out fish, they bite, and then you know where they are. Understand?"

"I think so."

"You my fish."

Can he actually be saying he was orchestrating the whole thing all along?" I don't understand," I said. "I stole the recipe from you."

"Did you?" he said. "You think it accident a window left open and a ladder outside? Why you think I show you the flash drive with recipe on? I know they scare you, make you get the recipe. I make it easy for you. I use you to, what we call, 'double stake' use you for wife and to flush out bastards who try to steal my recipe. You might have delivered on one. Who would have thought you good on both?"

My world just fell apart. This motherfucker was behind just about everything. I started to feel groggy. Tired. I felt pissed. "So, either way I'm fucked?"

"Yes. You are and will be like you say, fucked." Then he started to laugh. Not a happy laugh, a vindictive one, a laugh of joyful malice.

"You motherfucker," I shouted. I was so angry, I didn't give a fuck if the phone was recording. I shot forward at

Stadnyk. I wanted to kill him, smash him to pieces, but you don't get to be a mafia boss by being a pussy. As I shot forward, Stadnyk was lightning fast and blocked my punch. He countered with two massive blows to my neck. He grabbed my throat, I grabbed his arm. Though old, his arm was hard and powerful. He punched me again. "You feeling dizzy yet boi?" he snarled in my face. Why am I being called boi again?

I was feeling dizzy though. I felt like I was about to sleep. The vodka must have been spiked. "Your nightmare is not over. I'm not finished with you yet little boy." He threw me back onto my seat. Stadnyk was powerful and fast. He punched me again, and again. His face was full of a sadistic joy. He beat the consciousness from me.

# 12

## The End.

I woke up. I wasn't dead. What else could that mad fucking Ukrainian want with me? I tried to stand but my hands were cuffed behind my back. This was becoming a bit of a habit. I was in Stadnyk's office again, but what little furniture there was except for his desk had been moved to the walls. Then I noticed what I was wearing, a shiny white lycra body suit with gold piping and golden swirls. There was plastic sheeting on the floor, and that didn't bode well at all. I struggled and got up. My feet were shackled together by about three feet of chain. My ass was cold, I looked over my shoulder and saw that the lycra suit had no rear. My buttocks were out. I was bare arsed. This was very not good. I looked like a gay porn version of Elvis. What the fuck had I got myself into now? Around the room were tripods, reflectors and lights, it looked like a movie set. So, they are here to film something and I'm pretty sure I heard the sadistic rape of a guy here before. I'm in an assless jump suit. Clearly, my situation had not improved. Okay, so

I kinda was prepared to die, but not like this. I didn't want a sausage roast beforehand.

"Well well, look who is awake," Stadnyk said as he walked into the room. "Our little movie star." Stadnyk was in a large towelling dressing gown, below it he had bare feet with cherry red painted toe nails. "I've called the police, they will be here any second." I shouted.

"So what, you are telling me too hurry up, fuck you fast yes?"

"Nooo. I mean let me go and I will keep quiet."

"You know I cannot do this. You know too much. You will die. Right here, tonight. It will be painful, but thank you for telling me to be quick yes."

Under the circumstances, I think I'd rather it was quick than have him take his time.

Stadnyk dropped his gown. His brick tanned body was muscular and sculpted, a surprise considering his age. A large leather harness crossed his chest and was fixed to a dog collar. Each nipple had a big ring through it's flesh and a chain from them fixed to the dog collar. His bottom half was exposed but for a studded leather cock ring, painfully bunching his balls and erect penis together. Trapping the blood so it bulged bright red, all bumpy and shiny. It looked fucking horrid.

"You like?"

"Fuck no."

Stadnyk stepped closer, he gently felt my cock through

the lycra suit, then head butted me in the face. Splitting my lip. Bastard, my mouth is going to look like the lips of his dead wife's cunt at this rate. I reeled backward and almost fell over because of my shackled feet. "You know, I almost make as much money from my snuff movies as I do from drugs. You would not believe but supply follows same route as drugs. Convenient no?"

Stadnyk walked to the door and called out to his accomplice, "Uri, table, we must be fast. He wants fuck quick!" He started humming a happy tune, looking at me grinning, while he fondled his cock. Uri, the massive driver aka to me as Mr Enormous, arrived wearing a similar cock adornment, but in a little bra and a Nazi hat. He was massive, hairy and muscular. For a second I couldn't help but be in awe of his freakish oversized muscles, he was like a giant porn gorilla. His cock was enormous too. It looked like a bodybuilders thigh. That made me sweat, the thought of being arse raped was bad, but Uri's gigantic cock would just destroy me. I thought about telling him to use some margarine as recent experience had taught me it helps in such situations. Uri brought with him an upright table on a stand. It had hydraulic legs so it could be rotated horizontally or vertically on its axis. There were two stirrups and a large person sized u shape cut out of the surface so it formed the shape of the letter X. It was without question, a table designed for rape. As he dragged it in my eyes followed him and I could see my clothes, thrown in the corner, Justin Bieber cap on top of them. Please God, I thought. Please someone be listening. Let Lorner have got my message. I hoped that someone was on the way to rescue me.

"It 's funny," Stadnyk said. "The things people will do for a chance to not die. Would you like a chance to not die tonight?"

I knew he couldn't let me live. "Fuck you." I said.

Stadnyk laughed. "No mister man. I think you find its fuck you." I could tell he was getting more and more excited and aroused by looking at his swelling Eastern European penis. He was sadistic. Stadnyk leaned over me and said, "You smell like fear." He then stepped on the chain between my legs so I couldn't back away and started to kiss and nibble my ear. He retrieved a remote control from his desk and pressed play. From somewhere behind me, Hushabye Mountain from Chitty Chitty Bang Bang blared out. Stadnyk, in his Ukrainain broken English started to sing along to it.

He opened a leather bag and removed a strap-on cock. I couldn't help but stare at it. It was shiny, flesh coloured and huge. He rootled about and got a lipstick out, looked in a compact mirror and applied it to his mouth while he sang. With badly applied crimson lipstick over his mouth and teeth, he approached me again. He smiled as he drew a smiley face on the head of the strap-on cock. I recoiled and he punched me in the sternum. I collapsed on my knees winded. He hit me so hard it felt like he shattered my spine. He placed the strap-on cock on my forehead, and fastened it tightly in place, then lifted me upright and threw me over the desk. I slammed into it, grazing my hip and crashed to the floor, unable to break my fall because of being cuffed from behind. Uri had meanwhile erected the fuck table, and set about fixing in place thick leather straps.

"You know what a Uniporn is?"

"I'm not a unicorn you freak."

"No, I say Uni-porn. This is what I call you when you will do anything to survive. Total compliance. There is nothing like seeing the tears of a man slapped away by Uri's large testicles, as you fuck his ass with that face cock you now have." He thinks I am going to fuck Uri's ass with the cock on my forehead, so I can see everything? Through my tears? No way. "Fuck you. I will never do that, you can go to hell."

"You will do it. They all do when there is a glimmer of a chance to live. You want to know how you will die? You will be exhausted from blood loss. This from the internal injuries sustained from Uri's beautiful, giant, Ukrainian cock." He reached out and stroked it. "Then he will sit on that dildo on your face and suffocate you with his testicles."

Murder by ballbag. Nice. What a way to go! Who the fuck thinks of these things? How fucked up and bored must you be to have to need to do this.

Uri removed his Nazi cap, and pulled a shiny black pvc zip up gimp mask over his head and then put the cap back on. "Forgot anything?" Stadnyk said to him.

"Hmmmmm hmmm," Uri replied with a shrug.

201

"Darlink," Stadnyk said. "You silly sausage, the cameras?"

"Hmmmmmmm," said Uri. He turned and left down the stairs.

Stadnyk Started Hushabye Mountain again. "I get so dehydrated from fucking, must drink much yes." He walked over to his drinks cabinet, to the collection of bottles and glasses and chose a drink. Then I saw it, the bottle he had selected. Just like Stadnyk said, I saw a glimmer of hope. I got to my knees, and then managed to get up right. I have the strangest kind of luck I thought.

Stadnyk had selected the ornate bottle that once contained the expensive apple juice, but now contained my piss from when I took a shit in his office. I was amazed how dark my piss looked. It did look like his apple Jews. Even if I can't escape, I'll have watched that fucker drink my piss. He placed a large tumbler on the desk, and filled it almost to the top with my urine. "Hurry up Darling," he crooned. He walked back over to me, drink in hand. Just drink it I thought, just drink my piss. But he carried on serenading me.

Just drink the fucking drink.

He lifted the glass to his mouth. *"Wave good-bye to the end of your life."*

"Beautiful song you think?" I play again. He walked over to the desk and started the song again from the remote control. An inch from my face and looking into my eyes as he sang to me some more.

Just fucking take a drink.

Stadnyk placed the glass to his mouth and gulped it down. He swallowed three times before he stopped. Cheeks bulging from the fluid within. He looked confused, then looked at the glass. He then looked at the bottle. Then he saw my smiling face.

"That's right fucker, your drinking my piss!" As I said, I have the strangest kind of luck.

Stadnyk spat it out and dropped the glass. He looked like he was going to throw up. I dived forward, violently swinging my head. The dildo swung wildly and smashed into his face and caught him by surprise. I swung back and the thick cock connected again, sending him reeling backwards. I sat down, spying his leather cuffed, bright red, baboon like balls and kicked out with both heels as hard as I could. My feet violently smashed his balls and he shrieked out in pain. Stadnyk dropped to the floor, face glowing red from pain so I kicked out again, my heel striking his chin and again his testicles. I managed to get to my feet as Stadnyk slumped backward. I stamped down on his balls again and again. Then jumped up and landed on his sternum. Well, he'd started the sternum thumping. I felt ribs crack and bone give under my bare feet. I knelt on his chest and said in his ear, "Not quite the kind of getting fucked by the cock on my face you were thinking of huh, you sick cunt."

I ran toward the door just as Uri topped the stairs. I caught him unawares, he had a large camera case in each hand

and could not defend himself. He just stopped in shock and shouted "Hmmmnngh mmmnngh," through the zipped up mask. I jumped up and kicked out at his face with both my feet. I hit. As I landed on my back I could see Uri flying backwards down the concrete stairs. The metal cases let out a deafening roar as they crashed down with him.

I wasted no time. I was right behind him. I didn't know how many men were downstairs and I didn't want to. I stopped at the foot of the stairs where Uri was. He was moving, but dazed, so I stamped on his monster cock and balls. I was getting good at this. "MMMMMMMMmmm!" The muffled scream stopped when my foot was wet with blood. I stamped down on his giant ape body and shiny black pvc head, then I ran.

I was out of the door running as fast as my shackled legs would carry me which wasn't very fast. I kept trying to look over my shoulder as I went, thinking they were coming after me. The large rubber cock on my face flapped about. At one point, I turned to look back and the fucking thing bounced down and smacked me in the eye like a solid fist. It hurt like a bastard. My eye instantly started to close over. Once again I was in the bright lights and bustle of club land. Running for my life. Pavements full of people laughing and clapping at me. "Ha, love it, you can see his ass," one guy shouted.

"Dick head!" said another pointing as I hobble-ran past them. One good thing about club land is that there is always a police presence. Through all the jeers and taunts, I found a police van. "Help me," I begged.

The van was full of uniformed officers waiting for the bedlam and violence due later. One officer laughed and told me to fuck off. I rammed the van, the cock on my head buckled against the window as I screamed, "HELP ME!"

The window descended and an angry looking policeman said "What is your problem sunny? Any more of that shit and I'll arrest you."

"Good," I said. "You need to call Detective Lorner at SOCA, or Detetive Cuvlum, call anyone you like, but fucking help me."

The policeman looked amazed, then looked concerned. "Get him in the van."

# 13

## The Police station – again, so not the end.

Once again I am in the police station, in the same room used by Cuvlum and Short for their interviews. It was all too familiar. However, this time I was there voluntarily and that meant I got coffee. A sergeant in uniform was trying to get answers and was trying his best to interview me. My head cock had been cut free leaving an impression in the skin of my forehead. I had a blanket for dignity.

"You want to tell me what this is about?"

"I will only talk to Detective Lorner. Have you called her?"

"She is busy right now. You will have to talk to me."

"No," I said. "She is busy now because she is looking for me. You need to tell her I am here. Besides, I will only talk to her."

"I have put in the call sir," he said. "How did you get the black eye?"

"I did it myself. Just get me Detective Lorner please."

"You punched yourself in the eye?"

"No, I did it with the strap-on cock. Get me Lorner"

"A strap on cock? How long was the cock sir?" The sergeant looked baffled.

"It was on my head, I was wearing it on my head. Get me Lorner. Please, make the call."

"On your head? *WHY* was it on your head?"

"Because I was being a uniporn."

"A Unicorn?"

"No, Uni-porn. Look, I don't mean to be rude, but I am not talking to anyone but Lorner. Please, this is an emergency." I felt safer in the station but worried for Bulldog.

The all too familiar buzzer sounded and a uniformed officer came in holding a portable phone. He held it toward the sergeant. "You need to take this."

The sergeant took the phone to his ear. "Yes," he said, then, "Yes, he is." He shot me a look and held his gaze on me. "He is still here and said he will only talk to you. No. He seems fine but for some superficial cuts and bruises." He cupped the phone and asked, "Are you okay? Are you in any pain? Do you need to go to hospital?"

Okay, do I need to go to hospital? Let me think. I have two badly abraded testicles, a penis with a ruined tip, my lip has been split multiple times. My eye has closed over from the impact from a solid plastic cock. And maybe the swelling wasn't from the impact. I have serious questions about how hygienic the dildo was. I mean, I might have an infection from stale ass juice. I have a blistered foot, that's bleeding badly and I think I have some major internal injuries such as a damaged spleen. One eye looks like a tomato and I have enough swollen lumps on my head to be mistaken for the elephant man. Don't get me started on the mental and emotional damage. "I'm fine," I said.

"He says he's fine. Okay I'll tell him." He terminated the call and looked at me, and for once I was viewed without suspicion or malice. "Lorner is on her way here now."

I didn't have to wait long. My eyes were heavy and I knew sleep was majorly overdue. I was exhausted and now that my body wasn't feeding on adrenalin, I was growing sleepy and hungry. If I shut my eyes, I would sleep for days. Each blink became laboured. A few coffees later and the buzzer sounded, acting like an alarm clock, snapping me from a semi sleep day dream that might have been hours long. Two plain clothed officers and Detective Lorner entered the room. Lorner's big, beautiful brown eyes had a genuine look of concern and care, like she had just found a puppy hit by a car. "Oh my God, I can't believe your alright. Do you need anything? Have you seen a doctor?"

What was wrong with me? My eyes got shrink wrapped in tears and I had a lump in my throat. I had to try my hardest to not cry. Why was I about to cry? "You got my message?"

"We got everything. Thank you. That was incredibly brave."

"Incredibly brave," echoed one of the plain clothed men. He shot out his hand to shake mine. I held out my hand and we shook. Then he looked at my torn up fingers. Lorner also looked at my hand. "Are you sure you don't need to see a doctor?"

I was about to cry again. Brave? Me? "I think I am okay," I said. "Everything?"

"Yes, your phone call from the car, we have all of that recorded as evidence. " She opened a plastic case and retrieved my cap. "This was a very smart move. Who knew that Justin had a purpose on this planet? I want you to keep it as a reminder of all that you did for us. It worked, it recorded everything."

I took the cap, inspected the gaffa tape bug and placed it on my head. "All that I did? I'm not sure I follow?"

"Stadnyk is in custody because of you. You hurt him pretty bad but we will over look that. We have his drug operation, we have him for murder, attempted rape and the production of snuff movies. We have his supply and distribution network. You pretty much handed us the whole case."

"What about Jay?"

"Jay Lowe?"

"Yeah did you find him?"

"We found him. He's dead. He'd taken a bullet in the back of his head." She looked pleased, "A professional hit. Close range."

"What?" Poor Bulldog. I tried everything to save him. "He was my friend. My only friend and I got him killed. Why? Why do you look so happy?"

Lorner shot me a confused look. "Hey, Jay Lowe was in

209

this from the start. I don't know what he told you, but he was an evil and a very violent man."

"No way." I was not going to let her ruin Bulldog, not after all we had been through. "No way was Bulldog violent and evil. He was a good guy and now he is dead and it's my fault."

"Who?" said Lorner.

"Bulldog, that was his nickname, that was how I knew Jay." I was in pieces. It had all been a waste of time. I had got him killed after all. Everything was pointless. I could imagine him there alone in the dark when they came for him.

"Wait here," Lorner said. Like I had a choice. "I have someone I want you to see." She went to leave.

"I don't want to see anyone now. If it's that creepy doctor guy or a grief councillor then they can fuck right off." The buzzer sounded and she left. Soon I heard the door open. I didn't look up. I didn't want to look at anything pretty any more.

"Dude?" a voice said. I looked up, and there was Bulldog. My Bulldog.

"DUDE!" I was so happy, "They told me you were dead."

"Who told you I was dead?"

"These people." I pointed to the police in the room.

"No," Lorner said. "We said Jay Lowe is dead."

"The singer?" said Bulldog.

"No. You," I said.

"They said Jay Lowe."

"You're Jay Lowe."

"My Jay Lowe? I wish Jay Lowe was mine dude."

"No, you are Jay Lowe aren't you?"

"Do I fucking look like Jay Lowe to you?"

"Who the fuck are you then?"

"Colin Churchill. Your telling me, you don't even know my real name?"

"Oh. So, your not dead then?"

"No."

"Can someone tell me what the fuck is going on? Who the fuck is Jay Lowe then?" Okay, so Bulldog wasn't dead. And that was good, I got something right.

"I will try to explain," said Lorna. "I'll get you another coffee and something to eat. We have a lot to go through while its still fresh in your mind. Your friend needs to go and finish his statement with the other officers now." Bulldog was walked away and he shouted that he would catch me later and to hang on in there. As the door shut I heard him yell "I love you man!" from behind the door.

"I love you too man," I shouted. "I love you too."

"You look hungry," Lorna said.

"I am."

"What would you like? Anything you want, it's on us."

"Anything?"

"Pretty much. I'll send out a squad car to get it," she said with a smile.

"I'd like a foot long veggie pattie from subway, with chillies and low fat mayo. Please no margarine."

"Veggie?" she looked shocked.

"I might be an asshole but I love animals."

Lorner took me through everything as I ate my sandwich. "The Chemist, who developed the scentless and undetectable cocaine had sold the recipe to Stadnyk and to Rob and Jay Lowe. The Lowes are a London crime syndicate. Now this caused a bit of a turf war selling to both. Both sides wanted to kill off the competition."

"Wales and sharks," I said.

"Pardon?"

"Oh, it's a gangster term," I said, trying to sound cool. "Please go on."

"We have been after Stadnyk and his operation for many years but he was impenetrable. We were also aware of the growing and ever violent Lowes. The Lowes seemed to be one step ahead of us every time. When the Chemist went into hiding, all parties went underground, we lost all intelligence on them. Then you came along."

"I'm sorry, I don't follow?"

"Okay, you will probably get very angry at us, at me. But I want you to think of the bigger picture here. The grater good."

"I'm still lost," I said.

"Please try and see this from our point of view. You turn up out of the blue at the Chemists house. The Lowes think you are the Chemist, and try to shake you down. Stadnyk knows you are not the Chemist but uses you as bait to get

212

to the Lowes. He also uses you to blame for the murder of his wife. He could do this only because he had leverage on you."

"The rapes?"

"Yes." Lorna sounded all matter of fact.

"But I didn't do the rapes."

"We know."

"What do you mean 'we know'? What was with all the wanted posters and the stuff on television? If you knew I didn't do it, why ruin my name? I have family and friends you know."

Lorner sipped her coffee and looked ashamed with herself. What followed sounded awful. "It was a gamble. No, that's not fair, it was more of an educated guess. We checked up on you. You've not seen your parents for nearly seven years and by your phone records you have no friends. This was all done under the guise of a rape enquiry. But to clear things up for you, your DNA profile didn't match that found on the young girl by the football fields. Your transvestite friend recovered from her coma and was quite happy to not get a conviction for attempted rape herself. She told us everything. As for Stadnyk's wife, we already had you under surveillance, so knew you couldn't have killed her. We were watching you at the time she died and were aware of the time you performed the sex act on the then deceased Leigh-anne Stadnyk."

Oh God, she said sex act. "Tell me, would you ever date a guy who performed a sex act on a large, dead, disabled woman?"

213

"No," she replied. I nodded wisely to suggest 'thought as much.'

"You brought everyone out into the open. You were like a wonderful gift, and, thanks to you, we have Rob Lowe and Stadnyk in custody. There are a few things we still do not know, but we will. And soon."

"So why did Cuvlum say Bulldog was Jay Lowe?"

"He didn't. He asked you what you knew about Jay Lowe. You assumed it was your friend."

"Who did Jay and Rob Lowe work for?" I asked.

"Nobody. They were the cartel."

"That can't be right. When I was with them and it all went to shit, it all happened because they took a call and were told I was still bugged. They called who ever it was on the phone Boss."

"We are looking into that, and it's a bit of a concern."

"Does he hate me? Cuvum that is, because he put my shit in his mouth."

Detective Lorner started to laugh. She was even more beautiful when she really showed emotion. "Don't you worry about Cuvlum, he's fine."


There was a stack of paperwork and statements. It would entail many visits to the police station, but I didn't mind that. It meant seeing detective Lorner. I knew I had no chance with her but there was something about her that made me feel like everything was worth the effort. A bulletin would go out on the television saying I had nothing to do

214

with the rapes. I felt like I had turned a corner. Things felt much better and I wanted to track down that old guy from the bridge and tell him he was right. He was fuckin right.

A police car dropped me home. It felt like a lifetime since I had been in my flat. I opened the door found that my humble abode had been occupied by an evil stink. Even though it was late, I opened every window and let the place air-out while I walked to the shop to get groceries and charge the electricity key. I even bought cleaning supplies for the first time in my life. I was going to sort out my flat and my life.

I got back and scrubbed and washed and vacuumed. I felt as though I was washing away the filth that had become my life and was slowly revealing a fresh, clean me. The bleach burned the open wounds on my hand, but it felt good. It felt honest. I looked at the new skin beginning to grow from within the dried blood, and it felt like there was still some of the me from before the time the ketamine, cynicism, depression and heart break took over. A rebirth. Like when an ugly caterpillar crawls into it's cocoon and metamorphoses into a beautiful butterfly. Okay, that might be some stretch of the imagination. I'd be a fuck ugly butterfly but I stand by the metaphor. Rubbish was bagged. Old, used and dried up condoms joined the socks that had become solid and the take away boxes that had married the carpet. I scrubbed and cleaned till the early hours. I'd even bought plug in air fresheners. I went to the kitchen, and there was the cow cookie jar.

I had discovered I loved life. Being so close to death, you realise how much dull stuff can be beautiful. How you can be almost Zen like, enjoying having nothing to do. I took the ketamine and speed from the jar and flushed them down the toilet. I finally stopped as the sun was rising and I climbed into bed. A bed with clean sheets. It was bliss. I wanted to review and try to understand the last few days but sleep came before I could resist. Morning came even faster. I threw open the curtains and it was a beautiful day. Things had finally taken a turn for the better. I boiled the kettle and made a coffee in my now spotless flat. I set the mass of paper work on the counter, statements and details for Detective Lorner. I took my Justin cap and put it on my head. A memento. Something to give the grandchildren. Today felt like the first day of the rest of my life. A knock at the door stopped me in my tracks. I looked through the window to see who it was. It would be a while before I lost my nervousness, even though I knew that crime lords tend not to knock on doors. It was detective Short, Cuvlum's side kick.

"How are we doing?" He asked with a smile.

"Good now. Hey, sorry for all the shit. I don't mean the actual shit, I mean the stuff, the hassle. Can I get you a coffee?"

"No, I'm fine," he said. "There are a few loose ends we need to go through. Am I disturbing you?"

"No," I said. "I was just about to make a start on the mountain of stuff Lorner has given me."

"You haven't started yet? That's good. You have been such a great help to us, I was hoping you could fill in a few more details. A couple of specifics."

"Yeah. Ask away," I ventured. We both sat on my ex-shitty sofa.

"Do you know the encryption for the cocaine recipe?"

"No, I don't."

"But you *do* know where is the encryption code is?"

"I have no idea Detective Short. I know nothing about it to be honest."

"It's okay," Short said. His face sort of cracked a smile. "You aren't in any trouble now. We know you knew the Chemist, so you can come clean. You are in the clear but you must have talked about it."

"No," I said. "You don't understand, I didn't know him at all."

"So where did he keep his computer?"

"I don't know."

"Who sold the recipe to Stadnyk and Lowe? Was it you?"

"No." I was beginning to feel a bit pressured. "What is all this about? You know all this. I had nothing to do with anything."

"Sorry, but we have to be sure. So tell me again. Where is the encryption key now?"

He was trying to catch me out. "I don't know. I know nothing about it." Something didn't feel right. Hairs were beginning to stand up on the back of my neck. Short smiled again but there was something under the surface of that smile.

"Have you told anyone else about the recipe?"

"No. Look, I'm exhausted, I need some rest. I think you should go now." Maybe it was a hangover of the last days events but I was beginning to panic.

"Give me the encryption. If you can't give me the encryption, give me the actual recipe. The one on the disk was fake."

Something wasn't right for sure. Short was pressing hard.

"I don't have it."

"Give me the recipe."

"I don't have the fucking recipe. I know nothing about the recipe."

"Give it too me." Short started to look menacing.

"It was you wasn't it?" I said.

"What was me?" Detective Short looked a bit taken back by my question.

"Who rang when I was with Jay and Rob Lowe at the barn. You told them I was still bugged. You were who they called Boss."

Detective Short looked at the floor. His head dropped, a swaying became a 'yes' of a nod. He was quietly laughing. "Clever boy," he said. "You would have made a good copper if you hadn't been such an asshole." Short withdrew a gun from his jacket and pointed it at me. The gun looked the same as the thugs, compact and mechanical. He then took his phone and dialled a number that was quickly answered. "Okay, now please." Never before had such innocent words sounded so ominous.

"Was Cuvlum in on this or is it just you?"

"Cuvlum? The man is a bafoon, an idiot. No, I have grown my own empire from many long years of knowing who, what and where. I'd love to say it's because police salaries and pensions are low. Have some ethical reason. But the truth is, I'm greedy and I'm an evil bastard." Two men came into the flat. The bastard must have put the door on the latch as I lead him in. I recognised them. Now smartly dressed, they were two of the men from the barn shootout. One of the guys opened a bag and started to scatter little pieces of tin foil with scorch marks, balls of cotton wool and syringes around my bed. Drug paraphernalia. He opened the bedside table drawer and placed foil in there too, some wrapped around solid objects the size of marbles.

"Stop! I've just tidied this flat. What are you doing?"

"Tying up loose ends. That's what you are." Short struck me on the side of the head with the butt of the pistol. The impact from the cold steel rattled my already loose teeth. From behind, the other thug grabbed me, forcing a wooden spoon in my mouth. Detective Short removed one shoe and the accompanying sock. The thug who was distributing the foil stood beside Short and handed him some pliers. Short held the large, rubber gripped tool in front of my face, opening and closing it. I tried to scream for help, but my mouth was gagged. The pliers crushed around my little toe. Short applied as much force as he could, destroying the soft tissue, then twisted it upwards so the bone and the joint shattered. Pain like lightning bolts shot through my

219

body. Unlike that sharp hit of pain from an accidental injury, this pain was deliberate and prolonged. Twisting the torn nerves free from the bone. I continued my muffled screaming. Short stopped and nodded to the guy at my mouth. The spoon was removed and I was wet with sweat. The pain had stolen my breath.

"Where is the recipe?" Short placed the pliers around the next toe.

"Please. I don't know. I know nothing honest. I don't know." I screamed out as the next toe was destroyed.

"Where is the recipe?"

"I don't know."


"You know, I actually believe you," he said, then nodded at the thug who had scattered rubbish about my room. "You were just an unlucky guy. Wrong place wrong time."

Short rolled up my trouser leg. My arms were grabbed and forced behind me. Short continued, "I like you. I really do like you. I think we could have been friends you and me. You are a funny guy. Shame I can't let you live."

"No please," I started to plead. "I won't say anything, I promise your secret is safe with me." A candle was placed by the bed and lit. A thug waited by it. Detective Short took from his inside pocket a foil envelope. "This is the purest heroin there is." He waved it in front of my face. "It's called Gold. So don't worry. It will be a lovely way to die. There is enough heroin here in it's purest form to kill a room full of people." He tossed it to the guy waiting by the candle.

"Please, I'll keep quiet. you don't have to do this. PLEASE!" I wanted to live. I didn't get one day, not even one lousey fuckin day to enjoy my new found love for life. Typical, I discover that there is much to live for and just as I do so, its snatched away. Life sure can be a bit of a bitch.

The golden powder was placed on the spoon. It hissed and bubbled as it heated, melted and boiled over the candle. Cooking above the naked flame.

"Please, don't do this." I started to cry. I begged. "Please."

A cotton ball was dropped into the spoon and the liquid was drawn into the barrel of the syringe. My begging was futile. I resigned myself to the fact that these bastards would not change their course of action. My begging became quiet pleads. "Please. You don't have to do this."

Detective Short grabbed my leg. It quickly became apparent why and it was clear that they had done this before. They were after the large and prominent vein in my foot. I made one last violent fight for freedom, to thrash my way free. To live. The men held me firm. My attempt to break free was a mere squirm. I looked on in horror. The needle punctured my skin and sank into my vein. A small amount was injected before the plunger was retracted, taking my blood into the chamber of heroin. Making a deathly dark red cocktail.

"No, no please!"

"Shhhhhhhh, everything will be okay soon," Short said. Slowly he depressed the plunger. I watched as the poison disappeared into my vein. Into my body. There was no escaping death now. I at last knew how I was going to die and it felt beautiful. A glow radiated out from within my stomach to every single cell and every nerve into the furthest reaches of my being. A welcome warmth that seemed to sing to my soul, caressing me from within as it grew. I let out a small groan as the cocktail kissed my brain. The overwhelming feeling from the drug was almost instant. I didn't care about anything any more, so divine was the sensation.

"Better than any orgasm isn't it?" Short said. "You can see why it is such good business." I just looked through half open eyes and nodded and grinned. My murder felt nice. "I couldn't let you live, or let you finish your statements. You understand that right? You will be found having died of a drug over dose."

"Okay," I said. Compliant. Putty. My toes didn't hurt anymore. Nothing did. Detective Short replaced my shoe. I said, "Thank you."

I was escorted outside, into a car and driven at speed through the town. My head slumped against the window. I felt truly blissful. If this is what heaven feels like then I can't wait to get there I fuzzily mused. Death felt really wonderful. The car weaved and swerved. It pulled up and Short flashed his badge to someone. Soon we were driving along a small lane in a beautiful lush green area. A park. "This is you," Short said.

"Okay," I replied. I tried to open the door but my hand felt like a balloon toy made by a clown. Short helped me out and walked me to a bench. He sat me down and said "For what it's worth, I am sorry." He returned to the car and they left.

The early morning sun on my face was warm, it made my skin tingle. The park was in bloom with flowers carefully placed by the council to bring vibrancy. I hadn't ever taken the time to notice how green grass is and how colourful flowers can be. All the effort by the gardeners had previously escaped me. I wanted to thank them for it. So there I sat, waiting to die. I was comfortably numb, my breathing slow. My stomach rejected the poison and I vomited, but even that felt pleasant. My death was taking longer than I expected, euphoria abated and my mood grew ever more sombre. I was alone. I fumbled for my phone. I wanted to call my mother before I died. Make things right. I scrolled through the phone and then remembered that I had deleted the number in a fit of temper a long time ago. I couldn't remember my parents home number. I couldn't remember anything. I needed to hear my mothers voice. I needed her to tell me that I will be okay. I noticed Mia's name on my tiny list. I called it. She answered. "What the fuck do you want?"

"Mia." I wanted to explain and tell her I was sorry, but she spoke before I could form the words.

"Don't ever try to speak to me again you bastard. Your

a waste of space. Never call me again. Ever." She hung up.

I scrolled through more names. Found Bulldog. He didn't answer. So I said, "Bye," to his answer machine. I needed company, just a voice, to help me pass away. I felt beautiful yet afraid.

I scrolled through more names and that was all that they were. A list of names. Not friends or family, just names of people who didn't care. They didn't really know me or love me. Nobody wants to die alone. I was free of physical pain but my heart ached. I wanted someone to hold my hand as I died, like on the films. I wanted someone to care.

My phone rang. I answered it. "Hello," I said gently.

"Where are you? We are coming for you. Hang on for a bit longer. Can you do that?"

It was detective Lorner. She was doing that thing she does when she pretends to care. "Do you know where you are?"

"Detective Short is a bad man."

"I know." She paused. "You did brilliant. The cap. We caught everything. Do you know where you are?"

"No. But it's nice here. I'm dying you know."

"Just hang on. Don't think like that."

"It's fine, really it is." My thoughts were hollow. "It's for the best."

"It is not for the best, just hang on in there. We are coming for you. What can you see?"

"It's pretty. Flowers, swings, a football field." My breathing

224

had grown slower. I had to steal spaces between the breaths to place my words. "Lorna can you do something for me?"

"Anything just keep talking. He's in a park," she shouted.

"Can you tell my mum and dad I loved them and can you tell Mia I'm sorry."

"You can tell them yourself. Just stay with me. I need you to look and see if you can find a landmark to help us to find you. Can you do that?"

There was a warmth between my legs. I looked down and a dark spot had appeared in the crotch of my jeans. It grew to the size of a plate. Steam rose as I pissed myself, heroin had made me lose control of my body. It had stolen my dignity. I hadn't realised I had any left to steal.

"Awww, I've pissed myself!"

"That's okay. Don't worry about that. I need you to find a landmark so we can tell what park your in. Can you do that for me?"

"No. Too tired. Going to sleep now. Night night Lorner. Lovely Lorna Lorner."

"NO, No. Do not sleep. Do you hear me? Keep talking to me."

Then I heard the singing. Beautiful voices. As if heaven forgave me and invited me home. I listened to the peaceful melody for a few moments. "I can hear angels. I'm going to die now, and the angels have come for me."

"I hear it too," she said. "They are not angels. You have to hang on for me. He is in a park near a church. I hear a choir. Come on people find me that park."

"Bye Detective Lorner. Have to sleep now. Really I do."

"You can't go to sleep yet. Please keep talking." The granite had melted from her husky voice and there was a detectable tremble in its place. She was fighting back tears.

"Hey, don't feel guilty, you did what you had to do."

I heard the sirens. My salvation, my last chance. "Hey, I can hear the sirens." But then the wailing made a key change as they sped past and disappeared into the distance. "Oh, not for me." My breathing became very slow. Gravity only affected my eyelids, trying to pull them closed, the rest of my body felt as though it would float away like a child's balloon.

"He can hear the sirens. You were right next to him. Go back!" Lorner was still shouting at people but spoke softly through the phone to me. "Talk to me, just keep talking okay?" Her voice broke and I think she was crying.

"Sorry for upsetting you. I'm sorry. Upsetting sorry. For you." Words were hard, I had to really concentrate to put them in the right order.

"I'm fine. Your fine. Just keep talking," she said. "Hey, here's an idea, when this is over I will take you to dinner. Not a subway, some place fancy, would you like that? A date. I know you fancy me, you sort of said it on the phone in your own little way. So just stay talking. Where should we go?"

People seem to have the need to speak the truth before they die. Confess all sins, absolve all guilt. Mine was more a statement of misery. "I feel like an ice burg," I said.

"What?" Lorner said.

"Like I've snapped off from the land and drifted out to sea. All cold and alone and I can't find my way back." I started to cry. "I'm so lonely." My speech was slurred.

Lorner started to cry. "Look, just stay awake. Keep talking. Don't you shut your fucking eyes, do you hear me? Don't you dare go to sleep on me." Sweet Lorner, she tried her best to keep me afloat. But, as she said it, I realised my eyes were already shut perhaps for always. "I'm so, so lonely. So tired and I'm so very very sad." Then words abandoned me just like people had.

"Keep talking. Don't you give up on me."

I wanted to keep talking but I had no words left. Just an empty head and a tongue that felt like someone else's.

Detective Lorner started screaming, "TALK TO ME, ARE YOU THERE? TALK TO ME DAMN IT! PLEASE, JUST SAY SOMETHING? Oh my god I think we've lost him..."

I dropped the phone. I could hear her screaming but she sounded miles away.

My breathing was laboured. I couldn't lift my arms. But sleep was so inviting, the darkness felt like Christmas as a child, fairground rides and love. It felt like home should feel, safe and secure. So with each breath, I surrendered my consciousness. I was sad and yet blissfully content. Fighting it seemed pointless, so I surrendered to death.

# 14

## Shitty luck bottoms out.

I scratched an itch on the back of my hand and it was slapped away. I opened my eyes and saw her big brown ones looking at me.

"How are you feeling?" Detective Lorner asked. I felt like hells asshole. I was in a hospital room, in a small room by myself, not on a ward. I had a drip in my arm and that was what I had been scratching. I was in a shitty looking pyjama top.

"I feel like boiled shit" I said. Lorner was about to reply when a doctor entered. He checked a little clip on my finger then ran his eyes over my chart and tapped my drip.

"You are one incredibly lucky man," he said.

"How do you figure I'm lucky? I almost died."

"Exactly. You should be very dead but your body was chock full of a drug called Naloxone. Can you explain that?" Lorner shot me a disapproving look.

"Naloxone?" I asked.

"That's right."

"Oh, well I had really bad stomach pains. And I thought I was going to die. I thought it was internal injuries and I couldn't take a shit for days. My friend had Gastric Enteritis once and was prescribed them. He gave them to me to help with my guts."

"Do you have any idea how stupid it is to take someone else's drugs?"

Lorner was giving me a hard stare, as was the doctor

"Yes, I know. Won't do it again," I said woozily. It's pretty stupid to take someone else's drug recipe too, I thought.

"How many did you take?" Odd line of questioning this I thought.

"All of them," I said.

"ALL? The whole box?"

"Yeah. With pain killers and scrambled eggs."

"Well, let me tell you why you are lucky. This is quite a remarkable coincidence. As you know, Naloxone, is used for the treatment of Gastroenteritis and other such conditions. However it has been found to counteract morphine given as pain relief. Naloxone is the number one drug used in America and Europe for the treatment of opiate overdoses. If we had got to you in time, we would have pumped you full of Naloxone to save your life. Purely by chance you seem to have self-medicated. Your stupidity saved your life."

"Well fuck me," I said. "I do have a shitty kind of luck."

The doctor returned my chart. Detective Lorner asked for us to have some privacy.

"I bet you have questions," she said.

"Did you know about Detective Short?"

"We suspected someone. The London cartel were always one step ahead. It had to be an inside job. Which is why we kept Cuvlum and Short in the dark."

"So, you used me as bait too."

"I'm sorry. I never knew or thought anything like this would happen."

"I almost died. I should have died."

"Not that it makes it better, but we thought who ever it was would be a messenger, not running the operation. I honestly had no idea your life was in danger."

"So am I safe now? Who has the recipe?"

Lorner, sat on the edge of the bed. Her body language relaxed. "There is no recipe."

"What?"

"It was all a hoax, a fake. There is no scentless cocaine. The Chemist was an undercover cop. Three years he spent selling to small time dealers like your friend Bulldog under the guise of a chemistry student. Three years pushing around the rumour of the scentless cocaine. Three years of court mandates and legal battles, inter agency fights, international collaboration. We had to get British and foreign customs to let samples go through airports undetected as proof. All one big theatre production to flush out two drug empires. It must have cost hundreds of thousands of pounds. And as it turned out, one of our own, Detective Short was working for the wrong side but he didn't know that the odourless coke was a scam. Then someone recognised our undercover officer. One rent boy into uniforms too many I think and we had to pull him. Everything was about to fall apart and you turned up. The cocaine was a fake so we had to come up with something they would want so bad they would break cover and fight for it. Expose themselves." Detective Lorner fiddled with her necklace and looked at the floor ."I'm really sorry that you walked in to it all and that you got hurt so badly."

"I forgive you."

There was a long silence, that wasn't at all uncomfortable. I was glad to be alive and it felt like she was glad I was alive too. Then she said, "I rang your parents, told them you were a hero."

"Did they believe you?"

"No. Your father said I was an actress and that it was some wild story you made up to make him think you were not a loser. Your father is an asshole."

"Yep. Your right there. Detective Lorner?" I asked.

"Yes."

I was grinning, "You owe me right?"

"Yes. Big time."

"Can I ask you to do something for me?"

"Anything"

"*Anything*?"

"Anything."

"You will do ANYTHING I ask?"

"Anything, I owe you that much."

"But you don't know what I'm going to ask."

"I know. It's still anything."

"Well, I was going to ask for a coffee, but, how about a blowjob?"

She was shocked but laughed out loud. "No way! Your feeling better then?" She collected her coat and bag.

"Just put the head in your mouth then, so it's not like a full blowjob?"

She laughed some more and it felt good. It felt like a real connection. Even though I knew I had no chance with Detective Lorner, she made me feel like I had thawed out. I was human again.

"Get some rest, I will come and see you later."

"Hey, you don't have to bother. I'll be fine. I'll come down to the station when I'm able and do the statements and stuff."

There was a pause. She turned in the doorway and looked at me. Our eyes met.

"I'd like that," she said. "Try not to kill yourself before then and only take the drugs the nice doctors give you."

"So, when you say you'd like that, does that mean you kinda like me?"

"No." She gave me a sly smile. "It means you are the biggest walking disaster to ever grace our station. You're like a celebrity down there."

She winked and walked out the door.

So, I thought, maybe I did have a chance after all.

The End.